Peter Hamilton was born in Newcastle upon Tyne in October 1960 to working class parents and was bred there. He has a passion for problem-solving and enjoys being challenged. He started to work in retail stores at the age of sixteen and has never been out of work since, and still continues to work full time. For many years, he has had a burning ambition of writing his own book and this first book is of a series of stories detailing the crimes solved by Lucy Spires, 'The Blind Detective'.

To my loyal and supportive wife, Michelle.

Peter Hamilton

LUCY SPIRES – THE BLIND DETECTIVE

AUSTIN MACAULEY PUBLISHERS™

LONDON • CAMBRIDGE • NEW YORK • SHARJAH

A CIP catalogue record for this title is available from the British Library.

ISBN 9781528935715 (Paperback)
ISBN 9781528998710 (ePub e-book)

www.austinmacauley.com

First Published (2020)
Austin Macauley Publishers Ltd
25 Canada Square
Canary Wharf
London
E14 5LQ

Many thanks to Wendy O'Connor, for her advice
and support.

Many thanks to Susan Walls, for the ongoing support.

Chapter 1

15ᵗʰ March, 9:30 pm

Detective Chief Inspector Lucy Spires relaxed in her deep hot bath, her five feet five, well-toned frame fitted neatly into the space; her long dark brown hair floated around the top of her bath; music drifted in from her bedroom from the local independent radio station, a mixture of random nineteen-eighties pop songs. The day had been a long and a stress filled one. This was her relaxing, chill out time. She could daydream and de-stress.

She managed a team of ten detectives, some of whom had been with her for many tears. She regarded the team not just as colleagues, but also as trusted friends. She supported them in every way she could. She also realised she had to be an agony aunt for all her team. All brought their problems, with relationships, family, pets, finances and every other thing imaginable. They trusted her, she was always there if any needed to talk.

The team worked well together, with a mixture of new inspectors, and also some established inspectors with a great deal of experience. She reported to the Chief Constable, he was a man she joined the North East Police force with the same month, the same year. She had no regrets in her chosen career. The past twenty-four years in the police force had gone so fast. During her time in the force she had risen through the ranks to her senior position through extremely hard work and dedication.

She also reflected on her failed marriage. She had fallen for a man she had known since her time at university. She really loved him, even though they were complete opposites.

Her idea of a holiday was two weeks on a beach or a relaxing cruise; his would be trekking through a jungle in South America, or a canoe going through river rapids. As time went on, they both realised she was already married to her work. The break up wasn't pleasant, but eventually they ended up as friends. They both promised to keep in touch with each other. He moved around doing a variety of jobs, from repairing roads to a ranger in a national park.

Time went by and contact between them became less and less. The last she'd heard of him he was in New Zealand working on a sheep farm; he had always loved the outdoors and fresh challenges. She was a little upset to learn he had settled down and was married with children. She would have liked to have had children. However, in the time they were married it didn't happen, and she had seen at first hand the issues brought with that; and it would have affected her work.

She had lost both her parents several years ago, her mother to breast cancer. Her mother hadn't just been a parent, but her best friend. She had supported her in every success and failure, never passing judgement. She always felt everyone deserved a second chance, although there were always exceptions. Two years after her mother passed, her father suffered a major stroke.

Lucy Spires was working fourteen-hour days. She was trying to find a missing person, an elderly man suffering from dementia. He was found near a lake where he fished with his grandfather when he was a teenager. Luckily, he was found alive and well, although very confused. Lucy Spires was very happy with this outcome. This sparked memories of coming home from work to find her father in his garden. He had passed away several hours earlier and he had died alone. He was her rock. He taught her to drive a car, after she learned how to ride a moped. She loved that time. It was precious; long summer days of fun and a few bruises and a few scratches from falling off the little moped. Every day she thought about them. She missed them so much. Her meals would be waiting for her when she got home from work, and the conversations about her day and her parents' days. She knew these would never return.

Following the collapse of her marriage, she had other relationships, but none lasted for various reasons. Difficult, time consuming cases meant her time was taken up. She couldn't give her commitment to a relationship it needed. She tried very hard to build relationships. She gave a lot of herself. Most would last for a few weeks. She enjoyed the company and physical side of the relationships. She had no specific types; she liked a good personality over stunning looks. She'd learned in her university days that the good looking, charming men were too often interested in themselves. She avoided relationships within the police force. Her father used to say, "Try not to mix business with pleasure. Don't bring your work home."

If she were in a relationship with another police officer, all they may have in common would be cases they worked on and this may cause a conflict. The hours Lucy Spires gave meant they would never go anywhere.

She enjoyed time on her own. Her position meant she was very busy, with contacting and speaking to so many people, departments, attending meetings; her working day was an express train ride. She commanded and received a great deal of respect from all her colleagues, having earned it with her dedication and work ethic.

Lucy Spires poured a glass of her favourite Shiraz. She picked up a thick file with the title 'Farooq El Haj. Confidential'. She had read this file many times. She wanted to go through it again as she had a meeting with her Chief Constable, James Ingram and with a director of the Crown Prosecution service, Thomas Archibald, at three o'clock the following day. This was a case she inherited from the previous Detective Chief Inspector, who had retired early with health problems. He had become too involved in the case and it led to him having a massive heart attack and staying in poor health. To get away from this case, he moved his whole family to the south of France. The case had been ongoing for almost two years. It had ground to a halt for almost six months, but once Detective Chief Inspector Lucy Spires took it over, it had developed to near conclusion. Another glass of wine poured, a packet of cheesy snacks opened in a bowl, she wasn't ready to sleep. She decided to make sure she had prepared thoroughly for the following day.

As she opened the cover, there were several photos of Farooq El Haj. He had been arrested five years earlier for assault. The police photos made Lucy Spires shudder every time she looked at them. He had an air of arrogance, modern hairstyle and thick black wavy hair. He wore expensive jewellery; all high carat gold; a ring on almost every finger and a very expensive watch. The photographs showed he was always smartly dressed, wearing handmade suits, handmade shoes. He had a reputation to maintain. The choice of vehicle reflected the amount of money he'd made; top of the range sports cars or expensive German saloons.

Turning over the dossier, it began: born July third, nineteen eighty, to an Afghanistan father & British mother. His father left the family when the young Farooq was thirteen years old. He went to work as usual and never returned. Searchers found he had used his passport to fly to Germany, and from there he disappeared. The young Farooq took this badly and rebelled at school. He was expelled several times for his bad behaviour. His lack of respect, particularly of any female authority, Lucy Spires thought must have come from his father's parenting skills. He was excluded from lessons for fighting and bullying. Other school children could be very cruel to a child with no father, being brought up by a single parent. Reading between the lines, Lucy Spires thought his mother had probably tried her best to bring him up through his difficult teenage years, but he was such an independent young man that he knew his own mind, and with no other person to keep him under control, he lost his way and became a man with huge issues, many now out of control.

At age eighteen he found himself joining the army. After the usual period of training he was posted to Afghanistan. As a fluent speaker of the language, he became a key member of translation teams, engaging locals in every type of communication. In his downtime, he tried to locate his relatives. He failed to contact or find any, but instead began to make contact with many of his father's countrymen. The type of industry within the country was not what he was used to. He eventually began to be aware of the illegal type of trades from the country. He quickly learned how the drug trade worked, along with illegal people trafficking. Over the next few years, he made many useful contacts. Learning all aspects of the supply chain, from opium growing farmers, who harvested the material to make heroin, to the drug lords who reaped in vast amounts of money, supplying across the world to anyone who wanted to buy it. These were the main players in this multi-million-pound industry. No-one paid taxes as corruption made the wheels turn. They had no morals, and as far as they felt, no-one forced anyone to push a needle into their arm and if they didn't supply the drugs, someone else would.

Demand never slowed; it only grew. The more they could produce, the more was sold to fill the never-ending hunger, leading to vast amounts of money coming back and re-invested on developing ways to make more drugs, leading to more usage, leading to more money being made. A never ending, growing vicious circle, yielding vast fortunes, but had to be managed or would fail completely.

He built up a plan on how to use this knowledge once he had left the army behind him. Using the Afghan language fluently and having made the connections, he knew an easy way to make lots of money. He knew he must have had the patience to wait as he had a few years left in the army. During this time, he went out of his way to cement relationships with his new-found friends. He knew he had to gain their trust before he would begin making money in his future.

He was passed over for the whole of his eight years in the army for any promotions. His record had blemishes for his fighting and violence to all ranks. He had a reputation as a man with a short fuse. He seemed to feel free to use his fists to sort out any issue. Lucy Spires felt he was a loner, with few or no friends. On his leave, he would disappear, spending time with local Afghans. He told his superiors and members of his regiment he was trying to enhance the army presence and build friends in communities. In real terms, he was learning how to smuggle drugs and arms, and become a useful person in England to help bring in illegal immigrants.

He left the army, returned to England and he quickly began to identify how to use the knowledge of illegal trades learned in depth, starting with running prostitutes and low-key drugs. He quickly learned the trade of bringing into England illegal immigrants.

This was four years ago, when Lucy Spires had first come across Farooq El Haj. She worked for several years in vice. Even then he learned very quickly how to manipulate others to get out of potential charges and always had alibis, which couldn't be challenged. Lucy Spires always felt frustrated as this was one of the very few cases she had not managed to bring to a satisfactory close.

She felt Farooq El Haj's power, even then, stretched to have corrupt officers within the Police force. Who or how many and which departments, she did not know, but she knew she had to be very careful or this case would never become fruitful and become her biggest failure. Chief Constable, James Ingram, also shared her suspicions. Too many things had occurred, too many times knowledge of cases had stopped enquiries in their tracks. His alibis included spending a day at sea fishing, in the presence of at least four or five of his employees. A difficult alibi to break as all said the same details, times, the fish caught, and who did what. These fishing trips occurred when shipments of drugs entered the country. Lucy Spires had no proof; she learned of the shipments days after. Intelligence from various sources, including worldwide agencies, always filtered through seemingly after the event. This frustrated Lucy Spires a great deal.

Lucy Spires' meeting the following day included a piece of information only three people were aware of: Chief Constable James Ingram, Thomas Archibald of the Crown Prosecution Service and Lucy Spires. Inside Farooq El Haj's organisation there was an informer. The person was never named in any administration, nor if they were male or female, to protect them from serious harm. In truth, it was the long suffering, trophy girlfriend of Farooq El Haj. She was always referred to as X. Her name was Leonie Barker and she was groomed by Farooq El Haj to be a sex trade worker. A blond haired, very lean figure, big breasted woman. He was sure she would be very desirable to most men, willing to pay a premium price for her services. Before he introduced her to drugs and being used by men, he decided to keep her for himself. She was used by him as and when he wanted her. She hated when he sent a car to collect her, usually at short notice. She was expected to be available any hour of the day, any time. He never lived with her, but he liked to be seen with her. Most knew she was there for show, to keep up his persona as the top man in the area. She hated him for that. If she had to spend time with him, it was usually to impress other men in his organisation. She hated the sex. There was no intimacy and it was usually very rough sex; a humiliating, degrading time. Once started, she would wish it was over. It never lasted a long time; the deed was done by him, and then most times he left. She also knew his secret: he also used boys for sex. If anyone ever found out and he found out the information came from her, she would be made an example of his ruthlessness and he would take pleasure in her final humiliation. This was the main reason he would never let her leave. She had pinned her hope on having her life back. She was trying to learn as much about his business so she could pass it on to her new friend, Detective Chief Inspector Lucy Spires. She had found out dates of his latest drug shipment, due very soon. She also knew he recorded everything in written form. He didn't trust electronic devices. During his time in the army, he learned how these devices can track movements, be listened into, be hacked into and data retrieved. He was paranoid about anyone knowing how he ran and controlled his operations. She knew he was very keen on minute details. This how he controlled everything.

Lucy Spires made sure there was little ever written down in email or note form about X. Meetings were few so as to keep suspicion as low as possible. As his organisation grew, more people now worked for him, and he retained them all by fear. Once he had used them and he felt they would be of further use, he used severe bullying to keep them in line. He had a reputation as being ruthless.

If any of his drug dealers or pushers dared to step out of line by not paying up, or got greedy, he would set an example of them. A sound beating, but not too severe to seek hospital treatment, or stopping them doing their day to day business. He also knew information about all his employees. He used this to force them to carry out jobs they would never consider. His favourite was to threaten to have parents, children or partners either beaten to a pulp or worse. This also meant he would not miss any business done on the streets.

Reading this made Lucy Spires despise the man even more. He prayed on weakness. The fact most could stand a beating to themselves, but have a father or mother beaten severely was, to most, unthinkable. He had done this to a new member who had sold large amounts of drugs, kept the proceeds and disappeared for a few months. Once his father had been badly mugged and left hospitalised for weeks, the message was heard loud and clear.

On the unfortunate young man's return, he was seen around his local town, and then disappeared completely. The word on the street was he had gone on a fishing trip with Farooq El Haj, gone out to sea, but never returned.

Everyone knew he had been murdered by Farooq El Haj, however, no body, meant no case. Everyone used by Farooq El Haj had received the news and closed ranks for fear of reprisals. The informant had contacted the police in a roundabout way. She had walked into a police station to report a lost dog. She knew of Lucy Spires as she had seen her giving an interview about the drugs problem in the area on television. She felt she had to take a chance and begin a dialogue. Lucy Spires met her at various discreet places. She would meet at her gym, or country house spa. They were never seen in public, nor spoke on any phone. The next meeting was always arranged as they parted company.

She had realised if she left Farooq El Haj, no matter where she went, how far away she went, he would find her. She would be made an example of never to cross him. The information she passed gradually fitted into place and a solid case was being steadily built. The last piece of the jigsaw was to follow in a week. Farooq El Haj was bringing a shipment of drugs, pure heroin and cocaine, into the country.

The informant didn't know the exact date, just that the drugs were coming inside a shipment of handmade rugs and cotton fabric, coming from Afghanistan via Turkey. He was stepping up volume coming into the country as demand had grown and his dominance meant he needed more. Farooq El Haj was paranoid he wasn't going to get every penny of goods he'd paid for. He always met the shipment, checked the drugs himself, then took the shipment to his base to be recut and packaged to resell onto his network of pushers and dealers. He would check the quality. The drugs were mixed with other substances to enhance his profits. He had learned many ways to squeeze every bit of margin from every shipment.

Lucy Spires wasn't looking forward to the meeting the following day as she would need a large team of officers to apprehend all parties, from Farooq El Haj through to the dishonest crew on the ship, to arrest numbers of pushers and dealers. They now had names, addresses, details of a large part of his crime network. If any slipped through the net they would resurface and start the trade again. This would be a massive operation, which would also require using other police forces and European agencies. Her biggest fear was Farooq El Haj learning of the planned operation. She had purposely kept all vital information about potential dates and locations within a very small circle of colleagues. She had operated on a need to know basis. The resources needed would need a high-level budget agreement, but as far as Lucy Spires felt, getting this volume of drugs and ending the reign of a major criminal, putting him in jail for a long time and closing that chapter would be worth it. She looked at her watch; it was now ten fifty-five. She quickly went over things in her head. All the leg work was done. The only final things were the number of officers to be made available and the date the drugs landed in the UK. As she turned off her bedroom light, she checked her alarm, set for six-thirty. She hoped she'd done everything she could to ensure this case would be closed and successful.

What she hadn't realised was the network of corrupt police officers Farooq El Haj had on his payroll. This stretched from Afghanistan through Turkey to the UK. He either paid them for information when supplied, or they were blackmailed and in fear of reprisals on themselves or families. Farooq El Haj was kept well informed, even about the pending meeting the following day and had made plans to make sure it would never take place.

Chapter 2

15th March. 11:35pm

At the back of Green Trees Retail Park, on a cold, damp, light rainy night, one streetlight gave a little light so faces and outlines were a little hard to make out. The two sex working girls waited for their next client. A car pulled up and turned its headlights to sidelights as it stopped near the two girls. The passenger door opened a little, making the interior light illuminate. Both could see a white man with a cigarette in his mouth. The taller, blond girl walked toward the car; the passenger door opened further and she entered the car. The headlights were turned on and the car did a slow U-turn and drove slowly out of and around a bend, the sound of the engine fading away. Then the remaining girl heard the whir of a motorbike sound nearing. She thought *this is my last punter tonight, I'm too cold!* She had heard the sound before, and knew who it was and what he expected. The motorbike looked too small for him, she thought, as he turned the engine off and pulled it onto its stand. The small woman, dark brown hair a little wet with the rain, walked over towards him. She slowly knelt in front of the stocky man; his leather trousers were just above his knees. No words were spoken. This would have been his fifth time here in a few weeks. He pushed his groin toward her mouth, a condom covered penis. She took it into her mouth and began to rock her head back and forward, performing oral sex on him. A few seconds later, she heard him moan a little. She knew it would be over very quickly as he could never last more than seconds. She liked the fact he wore a condom. She detested the way some men forced their fluids into her mouth and all over her face. She knew these were often fantasies not done by wives or partners. She focussed on the money he always gave her without question. She knew he was having an orgasm as his thickset body jumped a little back and forward. It was over. She waited for him to move back as he had done each time before. He had always pulled up his trousers immediately, almost embarrassed at what he'd just done. A second later, she felt him lean forward and felt gloved hands tight around her throat. She tried to take a breath, but his grip got stronger and stronger. She tried to pull his hands away, tried to scream, tried to push herself away, but she could not get any breath into her lungs. She tried with every ounce of strength she could muster. She began to pass out, her body going limp as her arms fell to the side of her bent knees; the fingers on her left hand moved from a clenched fist to uncurl her fingers, then stopped moving. He squeezed her throat long after she'd passed out and knew he'd taken her life.

He rolled his head back and looked up at the black sky. The cold soft rain cooled his face. He looked down at the dead girl's bulging eyes, the white of her eyes a pink colour. He carefully pulled up his tight underwear, carefully keeping his condom on his penis; he'd sat through too many American crime series to leave any trace of DNA or any evidence pointing to him. He moved her head to look at her, he thought *another drug taking whore off the streets!* He thought back to when he was seven or eight and his mother used to lock him in his bedroom and 'entertain' her friends who paid her well. In his head, he could always hear the grunting, fierce moaning, noises he never understood, hear his mother screeching in pleasure. Occasionally, the men would finish with his mother, then he would hear his bedroom door unlock. The same man would enter his room and forced him to do things to them, or they did what they wanted to him. He sometimes saw his mother watching from the entrance, no emotion on her face. She just turned away and let the man carry on. At this young age, he knew it was wrong, but who could he turn to or tell about. He never knew who his father was. His mother had always told him he was an unplanned accident from a fling with a Royal Navy Marine. His childhood was tough, with an uncaring, abusive mother. He had to fend for himself some nights. There were nights he would return from school and there would be no mother or food in the empty house. The final straw was her final night of her life. She had entertained men three times. The second had entered his room while he could see his mother at his now unlocked bedroom. He tried to fight off a well built, alcohol smelling man, who pulled all his blankets off his bed and forced him, by beating him, to masturbate him. Following this he left him on the bed naked and he heard the familiar click as his door locked. He heard a knock on the front door of the house and footsteps coming up the stairs. Within minutes he heard the thumping of his mother's bed as they had noisy sex. A few minutes later, it was over. He heard muffled voices, laughing sounds, then the sound of two moving down stairs, followed by the faint sounds of glass bottles and glasses clinking. He wanted to be released. He made his mind up, then never again. He was now almost sixteen years old and he felt that he was a man. No, never again. He would stop this tonight. A few minutes later, the sound of a door opening downstairs told him the guest had gone. A click at his bedroom door meant he could come out of his room. He waited on his bed. He heard his mother open another bottle of alcohol; he guessed it was probably vodka.

He waited a further ten minutes. He pulled on his old pyjamas, went downstairs. His mother was drunk, her usual state at this time, almost ten o-clock. It was dark, quiet and cold in the house. He shook his mother on her arm. She didn't move, just rolled her head and a few garbled drunken words were uttered. He moved nearer to her head, to ask her if there was any food in the house as he hadn't had a meal for several hours. He tugged her shoulder. Her eyes were closed, her mouth wet with saliva. She slumped off the kitchen chair and onto her knees in front of him. She was so drunk he felt she would start to vomit; she usually did that after drinking heavily.

He stared at this pitiful sight in front of him. He thought that this person who calls herself his mother doesn't deserve to breathe the same air as him. An intense rage overtook him. He put his hands at the front of her neck and began to squeeze, harder and harder. She put up no resistance; the alcohol in her system had made her senses numb. She moved her arms a little, but by then it was too late. She stopped breathing, yet he still squeezed until his hands ached. He knew she was dead. He had murdered his mother. All the rage, anger, hatred had come to a point that he couldn't stop himself. He didn't know what to do. He just sat opposite her lifeless body.

He reached over and picked up the glass bottle. He filled his mouth with the alcohol and swallowed it. It hurt as it went down. He felt numb, no emotion; not sad, nor angry, just empty.

There were several knocks at the door. He ignored them. He knew he would never feel another man touching him, forcing him to perform tasks he detested. He knew he would never hear the sounds from his mother's room while she entertained for money.

It became very dark. Light from the streetlights showed the unmoving shape opposite him. He stared for a long time at his dead mother. He didn't know what to do. He felt very cold sitting on the floor of the kitchen, but remained very still. He wasn't sure what time it was. He picked up the vodka bottle, just under half full, and he drank it until it rolled from his hand, almost empty. After a few minutes, he felt unwell; his head ached and was spinning, and he felt sick. Rain on the kitchen window tapped gently. He tried to move, but felt tired, very tired, so he rested his head in his hands. A few seconds later, he fell into a deep, drunken sleep on the floor.

He woke to find a policeman standing over him. The local milkman had seen the pair through the kitchen window and called the police. He was taken to a hospital to be checked over. Alcohol poisoning had taken its toll. He was given fresh clothes and a large, hot satisfying meal. He never went back to the house. Social services looked after him. This was the first time in his life he was given compassion and felt safe.

The police were aware of his mother's profession and felt she had lost her life to a disgruntled punter. No statement was asked for or taken from the young man. The young boy was never considered a suspect. Her murder was never solved. He was moved around foster homes until he was seventeen. After that, he left to make his way in the world.

As he drove the heavily silenced motorcycle away, he thought that this was the third prostitute he'd killed in this way. He felt he had the power of life and death. He felt he had a right to rid society of scum, drug taking prostitutes who plagued his world. He felt he had the power of life and death in his hands and he would never be caught. He was far too clever for that to ever happen.

Chapter 3

Detective Chief Inspector Lucy Spires gradually woke from her sleep to the sound of her police mobile phone ringing. Picking up the phone, it took a second for her to focus. The screen said 'Number Withheld'. She knew it was her operations desk at the regional Police headquarters. After a quick intake of breath, she answered with her professional, "DI Lucy Spires."

After a second, a familiar voice spoke. "Good morning Ma'am, Sergeant Andy Harrison. Sorry to wake you, but we've had a report of a suspicious death. It's a female at the back of Green Tree Retail Park. Three constables and the forensic teams are on site. Will I show you attending?"

"Yes, I'm on my way," came the reply from Lucy Spires.

"Will you please contact DC Emma Harper and ask her to meet me there, she may need directions." With that she was out of her bed and quickly brushed her teeth. Her clothes were in an organised way to dress quickly. A navy-blue trouser suit, red polo neck sweater, brown boots. She was ready for the day. She grabbed a bottle of flavoured water from her fridge, picked up the Farooq El Haj file and her phone and handbag. She locked her front door. A peep from her car and she was on her way to the crime scene. The winter was her least favourite season. She hated the long dark nights and she hated driving in darkness, although this time of the morning meant traffic was quiet.

Lucy Spires knew exactly where she was going. The place was a common working area for sex workers. She had been to this location many times. She had got to know some of the girls during her time in vice. She also felt sad for them as almost all would never have chosen this as a career; most fell into this profession through desperation. Some worked independently, some were worked by men or women and controlled by them. Many had personal issues. She couldn't understand the types of men using these girls. They were from all types of profession, from builders to lawyers. Some highly paid professionals to foreign sailors.

As she neared the crime scene, she could see the blue flashing lights through the rain. There was a small crowd, some with mobile phones, trying to record what was occurring. She parked near the forensic van. She could see silhouettes of figures inside a large white tent. The rain was heavier now and colder. She lifted the wet slippery police tape, showed her warrant card to a small female officer, who greeted her with a nod. She had seen her before but didn't know her name. She walked towards the bright lights and white tent erected around the incident site. She heard voices she recognised.

"Good morning gentlemen. DCI Lucy Spires. What do you have for me?"

Two uniformed officers turned to meet her eyes. They both moved to the side and she could see a dark-haired girl, with her knees folded under her, her hair partly over her face. Lucy Spires drew a long, slow breath. She looked at the white suited forensic medical man; he was concentrating on making notes. He was a tall, lean, spectacled man. She had come across him before. She broke the silence and introduced herself to him. He pushed his glasses further up to the top of his nose.

"I'm the duty pathologist, Dr Seth Hall. We have a mid-twenties female. My prelim examination is that she was unlawfully killed, her life taken by strangulation. A full post mortem will, I think, confirm my initial findings."

Lucy Spires looked at the girl with pity and sadness; a terrible frightening way to lose a life. Her thoughts were interrupted as the medical man said, "I would estimate the time of death approximately around midnight. She is soaking wet through." He looked at Lucy Spire's face. "I don't think this is the first victim I have seen. I assisted in a PM a few weeks ago with similar marks, and by the looks of things, her killer took trophies in the same way."

Lucy Spires realised he was correct. She looked closer to the body and could see each ear lobe had a line of blood. The killer had torn out the earrings. She looked into Dr Hall's blue eyes; he had now taken off his glasses.

"Did he take the earrings post mortem?"

He nodded as he put his glasses back into his glasses case, which loudly snapped shut. "I've done all I can here for now, detective," said the doctor. He went on, "We'll take her to the Queen Ann hospital mortuary."

Lucy Spires stood upright and began to collect her thoughts and focus. "Doctor Hall, will you please let me know when the autopsy will take place. I would like to attend as I need to be up to speed with this poor girl as soon as possible, and if you are correct this could be his third victim. If so, we need to stop his fourth."

Again the doctor nodded in agreement. The crime scene photographer appeared at Lucy Spires' shoulder in a blue protective suit. Lucy Spires moved out of the tent into the cold; the rain was now a little heavier. She had a lot to do before her meeting with the Chief Constable and the Director of public prosecutions later that day. Just then, DC Emma Harper came up to her.

"Morning Ma'am."

Lucy Spires looked at her, she had been promoted to Detective Constable a few weeks earlier. "Good morning DC Harper. This will be your first suspicious death as a detective. You don't need to go into the tent. A full post mortem will have a report for you to analyse. I think they're finished here, they want to move the body."

They both looked at the tent. Every few seconds a flash from the forensic photographer lit up shapes.

"Ma'am, this is my first suspicious death. I have to start somewhere," said DC Harper. Lucy Spires looked at this younger version of herself.

"Of course, you are right, but it's not pretty," Lucy Spires replied. With that, DC Emma Harper cautiously moved one side of the tent and peered in. A few seconds later, she came out, her face looking a little red.

"Ma'am, she doesn't look like the other two victims. Her clothes are different and her shape is a little more rounded."

Lucy Spires was a little taken back. She had glanced at her clothes, but hadn't picked that up.

Never judge a book by its cover Lucy Spires thought to herself and turned to look at the bigger crowd gathered. "Now the work begins," Lucy Spires said quietly to herself. "DC Harper, have you got your notebook. There's several things I need you to do."

A quick flick of DC Harper's bag and the notepad was in her hand, pen waiting for instructions. Lucy Spires thought for a second, then looked at DC Harper. She was a little dishevelled and wet.

"Firstly," said Lucy Spires, "interview the person who found this poor girl. Secondly, try and get her identified. Look for her handbag or any means to find out who this poor woman was. I'm heading back to Headquarters. I'll find out the time of the post mortem. It's your first suspicious death as a DC. If you feel you want to be more of a part of it you should attend." With that she felt in her pocket for her car keys.

As she walked toward her car, a dark van pulled up, its windows blacked out. It parked. Three men in forensic overalls got out and brought a long black body bag from the back of the van. As she got into her car, she looked at the crowd in front of her and thought that this life was taken in the worst circumstances she could imagine. As she pulled on her seatbelt, she said to herself, "We have got to get this man before he does this again." She had a picture in her mind of the girl's face, her bulging eyes. She thought a terrible waste of a young woman's life, regardless of her occupation.

As she drove back to the police headquarters, she felt a little light headed. The meeting later that day and the extra work this new case meant the rest of the day would be stressful and manic. Around twenty minutes later, she was heading upstairs to her office to prepare for the briefing of her team on this latest crime. She already had the names of who would do what and how they would do it.

She went straight to the main 'Major Investigation Team' office. Her notes in hand, she went through to a buzz of voices, which silenced when she neared two large whiteboards. She had her team's attention. She looked at some of the faces. Some had been with her in the Major Investigation Team for several years and most knew what was coming their way. One of the detectives, DC Phil Henderson, appeared at her right side and handed her a coffee. She nodded in thanks. The team knew a little of the morning's events, but were waiting for a full, comprehensive brief. Detective Chief Inspector Lucy Spires went on to explain from her arriving at the scene, to arriving back to headquarters. All the information needed to begin this investigation had been given in a short fifteen-minute briefing. More details would follow following the autopsy of the victim later that day.

DCI Lucy Spires looked around at the individuals. Each had their strengths. She looked at a middle aged, round man; Detective David Evans. He looked as if his fashion sense was stuck in the mid-nineties. A softly spoken Welshman, married, with three small children. He'd been a loyal and dedicated team player for several years, and was very good with the leg work jobs.

"Evans," said Lucy Spires. "You know the area. Ask around. Who saw what, how did this young woman become a victim, how long has she worked that area, witnesses, the usual, please. Someone knows something, and we need to bring this man to book."

Another quick glance and her gaze moved to the gangly, gingered haired beanpole of a man, Detective Phil Henderson, her coffee bringer. Newly single, no fashion sense, but always smartly dressed. "Phil," said Lucy Spires. "I need you to look at CCTV. Look at the area footage. The location is the back of a busy retail park. Look for vehicles coming back and forth to the site. Check with our colleagues in traffic, see what you can come up with. This could be the key."

Just then, DC Marie Booth appeared from the entrance of the office. "Ma'am," she said. "We've had a positive ID on the victim this morning. A twenty-six-year-old single mother, has a daughter, will be five years old, Julie Anne Cooper. One conviction for shoplifting, stealing baby products. Received a community service order and fined."

Lucy Spires was lost for words for a second. DC Marie Booth went on to inform the team that family liaison officers had visited her address and spoken to her mother. They live in a council flat, mother is disabled, she has MS, and her own father lives in Scotland and is estranged. The father of the five-year old child is from Poland. He disappeared four months ago as he had a death in his family; he went back to Poland and never returned. State benefits claimed had stopped until the benefits agencies reviewed her applications. To make ends meet and keep her family under one roof and fed, she'd told her mother she was working in a taxi office, getting paid cash in hand. Sometimes she earned little, other times a lot. Her mother told her that when she comes in from working, she has a long hot shower. She tried to stay awake for her daughter finishing work, but she fell asleep as her daughter was late coming home last night.

Lucy Spires nodded in thanks to DC Marie Booth. A little murmur went through the team as they all collected their thoughts at this news. Lucy Spires took a deep breath. Her eyes met Detective Vicky Wallace, a thin, short, blonde haired, thirty-year old attractive detective. "Vicky, please go and re-interview Julie Anne Cooper's mother. Find out when she went to work, times, what she earned, what she wore when she went to work. How she got to where she was killed is vital. Was she picked up by car? We need to know everything about this girl. Did you get all that?" A very definite nod and she grabbed her long coat and mobile and was on her way out. Lucy nodded to the other members of her team, turned on one heel and returned to her office and closed the door.

Lucy Spires felt butterflies in the pit of her stomach as she realised the full impact of this poor woman's murder. She had gone on the streets to sell the last thing she owned to feed herself and try and look after her family. She was just about to ring social services to seek advice about the victim's five-year-old daughter and help for her mother when her office phone rang. The time of the post mortem was scheduled for midday. The home office pathologist was due then. She hoped they would be thorough and be able to give details of who committed this deed. She rang DC Emma Harper to tell her the time of the autopsy. She was very keen to attend. She then rang her contact at Social Services to arrange for the latest victim and her mother to receive as much help as they needed, both emotional and financial support. She relayed the information about the circumstances of state benefits being stopped and how they may need urgent help to get the family back on their feet.

Lucy Spires got out the files of two other cases of a very similar nature. One of three weeks ago, a sex worker called Elizabeth Jane Peterson, twenty-nine years old, heavily dependent on class 'A' drugs heroin and cocaine. Unlawfully killed in a very similar way at the Hopper Retail Park, twenty fourth of February. No evidence of DNA or fibres or hairs. There was evidence of sexual intercourse, but no matches of any DNA on the police database. The case was ongoing, but as the victim had lived alone, the case notes said she had worked the streets for several years to pay for her long-term addiction to drugs. Had been arrested four times, but had gone back on the streets the following day of prison release. Lucy Spires felt she had gone under the radar as a drug using prostitute. She still didn't deserve to lose her life in this way and deserved to have her killer brought to justice. There were too many similarities to dismiss, including the earrings taken from her. Lucy Spires wondered why these had been taken and why not the money this girl made. Why kill these women in such a brutal way?

The other file read along similar lines. An early twenty-three-year-old, white girl, drug user, a new sex trade worker, had lost a string of low paid jobs, caught stealing cash from a shop where she worked, was the last job she had, reported to the police, but the owner didn't want to press charges because he had felt sorry as she was stealing to feed her habit. The way she was killed was again too similar to not be linked. Again no DNA, no fibres. Nothing linked these brutal murders apart from they occurred behind New Bridge retail park, at known sex trade areas and on different days during the week. One on Monday, one on Tuesday and this one on Thursday.

Lucy Spires' office phone rang. It was DC Emma Harper. She was bringing coffee and had further information about the case. Lucy Spires asked her to come straight to her office once she got to police headquarters. Ten minutes later, DC Emma Harper was in Lucy Spires' office. Lucy Spires pointed towards the chair opposite her desk. DC Emma Harper sat down and looked at her confidently.

"I interviewed a man called Robert Williams. He was the person who found our victim this morning," said DC Emma Harper. She then got out her note book. "He at first stated it was the first time he'd been to this area, but I didn't believe him. He said it was a short cut to an all-night supermarket. He was going to buy cigarettes and coffee. I didn't believe this either. After pulling holes in his story, he told me he often visits the area to look at the girls doing their work. He is married with one child and another due in two months. He is a bit of a voyeur as he looks from a distance. Before he came across our victim this morning, he saw a car pick up a girl and drive away, leaving our victim by herself. He went to the all-night supermarket, bought cigs and a jar of coffee, came back fifteen minutes later. A black, very quiet motorbike was pulling out of the back of the retail park. He noticed it as it was free-wheeling, then the engine kicked in with a plume of oily smoke and was very quiet. He couldn't see the girl anymore so went back to work. His job is to do orders for an internet company. They received orders from all over the world for at different times of the day and night. His job is to pick and pack the night orders. He went back out for a cigarette to where he'd seen the girl and spotted her lying in the rain and called us. He is to come in around five-thirty to do a statement. No information on the motorbike as it was too far away."

DCI Lucy Spires, inhaled slowly. "Well done. We have a witness who saw a great deal, but not a lot of help. We do however have precise times. Once we get back from the autopsy, get the CCTV from the supermarket to verify his story and piece together a time line of events as they occurred." She was very impressed with the new member of her team. Not for the first time had she felt this young woman was a young version of herself, very committed with a keen eye for small detail. DCI Lucy Spires had never seen an officer make as many detailed notes. She never relied on her memory, in case any detail was missed.

With that, she glanced at her watch; it was eleven-twenty. "We need to get a move on. The home office pathologist won't wait for us," said Lucy Spires. With that, she spun her coat over her shoulders, drank the last of her coffee, picked up her handbag and they were off to watch the autopsy of Julie Anne Cooper at the Queen Ann hospital. Lucy Spires had bad memories of this hospital as both her parents had passed away there. At least they were going to the mortuary entrance, away from the bustle of public parking and traffic lights.

The ten-minute journey went smoothly, although in her windscreen mirror, Lucy Spires noticed a white transit van speeding up in the line of cars, and whenever there was a gap, the van would illegally overtake. Lucy Spires, in her unmarked police car, hated bad driving; impatient drivers taking chances was her pet hate.

The entrance to the hospital morgue was at the rear of the hospital, accessed by a service road, and used for deliveries to the main kitchens and medical supplies. A right-hand turn, off the road was on a blind bend. The traffic coming toward them slowed for the bend in the road. Lucy Spires pulled into the service road, parked near the entrance, put her 'Police on Duty' sign on the inside of the windscreen. DC Emma Harper was out of the car first. She looked a little pale. Lucy Spires looked at her and told her to keep quiet during the autopsy and if she felt faint or worse, to go outside in the fresh air, come back when she was ready and still be quiet. She explained there was no shame in feeling unwell on any autopsy, let alone the first one.

The home office pathologist had started. An assistant showed the two women to a row of seats behind thick clear glass, above the table the pathologist was working at. They sat quietly listening to Professor Richard Bradbury, home office pathologist's voice as he described the way in which he felt she was unlawfully killed. He went on to demonstrate how the offender strangled the girl with very powerful, strong hands, a very deliberate act of pre-meditated murder. There were traces of leather fibres under her small fingernails, and no traces of sexual activity. He went on to say there was no appearance of intercourse, no trace of male semen. He went on to demonstrate as he viewed it, the victim was kneeling in front, probably performing oral sex. He stopped and stood up straight. "I would suggest he wore a condom. This would negate the presence of semen. The bruises around her face show she tried to force his hands away from her. The pressure he used almost flattened her trachea. She would have remained conscious for less than thirty seconds. The falling blood pressure and lack of oxygen would have made her pass out. After that, death followed quickly. She would have been in no more pain." He paused for a few seconds. Lucy Spires was concentrating so hard she hadn't noticed DC Emma Harper was making notes as the Professor gave his detailed information.

After a further fifteen minutes, the Professor concluded his examination. He finished off by telling his small audience this was the third unlawful death on which he had performed an autopsy. He looked at the faces behind the glass and said, "I can only give you the facts, but this is now the third female victim unlawfully killed in this way I have examined. I can only hope the police force are doing their utmost to make this the last time I am called in." With that he turned in towards the body, peeling off his long, thick, blood stained gloves, then his plastic apron. The two women picked up their handbags. DC Emma Harper frantically finished off her notes, put her pen back into her bag and zipped it up.

"Well." said Detective Chief Inspector Lucy Spires "How was your first time here?"

DC Emma Harper, breathed in slowly, considering her answer. "Ma'am, the man who did this is an animal! We must stop him. I would hate to do this again, especially if the victim is a desperate single mother trying to make ends meet and feed her child." She stopped herself from adding to that as she felt a wave of anger against this man. The lights in the room were quite dim. As they came outside the bright daylight made them both take a few seconds to adjust to it.

Lucy Spires and DC Emma Harper looked at each other; both nodded they were okay. They came out of the building into the welcome fresh air. The smell of disinfectant seemed to cling to their clothes and in their nasal cavities. Both got into the car. Lucy Spires looked across at the young DC. The paleness had gone and she felt she had a new look of confidence about her.

"Well DC Harper," said Lucy Spires. "That was not a pleasant experience. After many times here, I still leave feeling humble and determined to solve each case. The hard work starts here. We need to collate every piece of this jigsaw, put it together and get this murdering bastard!" DC Emma Harper was taken aback. She had never heard her boss swear. As Lucy Spires drove to the edge of the junction, the traffic was heavy and fast moving.

A split second later, and before Lucy Spires could react, a headlight flashed her eyes. A second later, she heard a deafening noise as her car was lifted, twisted and pushed into the air. DC Emma Harper started to scream at the top of her voice. There were sounds of glass breaking, metal scraping and twisting. She felt a sharp pain in her right leg, above her ankle. She instinctively tried to move it, but it was jammed. A split second later a similar pain in her arm and her side made her feel like her body was on fire. During all this, the steering wheel airbag had activated. She had seen the white balloon flash into her face, then felt her head spring back as a piece of a metal came through the door window, smashing it into thousands of pieces. All went quiet. Lucy Spires tried to move and felt trapped. She tried to take a breath. Her chest was tight and she tried harder to take a breath. It felt even tighter. She felt an over whelming desire to sleep. She could taste blood. She slipped away as the need to sleep had taken over. Within a minute, a huge team of nurses and doctors were at her side. What they found was not pretty. Their extremely fast reactions saved her life, but at a massive cost.

Chapter 4

It was 35 days later when the hospital began to bring Detective Chief Inspector Lucy Spires out of her induced coma. She slowly began to wake up. The team of surgeons had just managed to save her life. The list of injuries included damaged internal organs, broken ribs, punctured lung, broken right wrist and broken right tibia. Bruises across her whole right-hand side. These were injuries surgeons could deal with and repair, the doctors could see them heal. The biggest and most complicated injury was a fractured skull. Pushing pieces of her skull into her brain, there was also a bleed on her brain. Until she was fully awake, the full extent of her head injury would not be fully understood.

Over the next few days, Lucy Spires began to breathe by herself, the oxygen mask was removed. She could feel her senses returning. She could hear a great deal of noise, voices, different male and female tones. She tried to move and sit up, but the hands of a nurse gently held her down. She spoke softly, "Welcome back Miss Spires, you will never know how lucky you are. Do you know where you are?"

Lucy Spires tried to speak, but her jaw was very, very sore. Her mouth was so dry. She felt something on her lips and a straw went between her lips. She sucked and felt tepid fluid wash into her mouth. She tried to swallow; it hurt a great deal. She craved more of this weak orange juice, but heard a male voice telling her to slow down as she had not taken any fluids since her accident.

From her left side, Lucy Spires heard a deep, Indian sounding male voice. "How do you feel young lady? You have been incredibly lucky." He gently picked up her left lower arm to feel her pulse. He continued, "My name is Mr

Harsha Singh. I'm one of the surgeons who saved your life. If you are involved in a major RTC, have it fifty yards from an Accident and Emergency department of a major hospital." He had a cheerful voice, Lucy Spires thought.

Lucy Spires took a deep breath and said, "Why is it so dark?" Immediately she could sense something was wrong, very wrong. Mr Singh placed her wrist gently down by her side. She could feel his breath near her face, his gentle hands moving around her face and touching her head. He moved his hand to the back of her head.

"Miss Spires." he spoke again, the tone of his voice now a little slower and sombre. "We need to do some tests, but I'm afraid there was damage to your head, specifically to the back of your skull. The vehicle smashing into your car caused your skull to be broken and fragments of bone went into your brain. This caused a bleed." He paused as he could see the change in Lucy Spires. He continued in the same tone, "There is no other way to explain this, we have tests to do. A lot of tests, so until we have completed them and had the results, nothing is certain."

Mr Singh sat on the edge of her bed and explained every injury she had sustained. The biggest injury she had was to her head. Mr Singh explained broken bones could be put in a plaster cast, or pinned and repaired. A brain injury was a lot harder to say how bad the damage could be. Lucy Spires moved her hand over her head. All her hair had been shaved off. She could feel a scar across the back of her head, ridges where her skin had been stapled. There was so much to take in. Lucy Spires felt tired, so tired. A familiar voice from a nurse asked her if she felt hungry, Lucy Spires just needed to sleep.

Several days later and physical strength returning, Lucy Spires was beginning to realise she would be totally blind for the rest of her life. The test results all came back to confirm her optic nerves were damaged beyond repair. From the second of the crash, her life would never be the same again. The feelings of despair were alien to her. There were times she wished the van crashing into her had just killed her. She was never a depressive type of person. She had always seen a glass half full instead of empty. Her outlook had always been positive. Her father often quoted his favourite saying, 'Tomorrow is a new day; the sun will always come up and shine somewhere!'

It was often the feeling of isolation she felt, not knowing what time it was, or see approaching doctors or nurses. She heard lots of strange voices, even in different languages. She had constant headaches and because her mind was in total darkness, she felt ready to fall asleep almost at any time of the day. She felt very lonely. Being an only child and having lost both parents, there was no-one she could reach out to for comfort or major support. The situation she had found herself in was at times unbearable.

Over the next weeks, Lucy Spires learned to walk again. Physiotherapists worked daily to help her regain her balance. Everything felt strange to her, from washing, to eating, to trying to dress herself. During her time in her coma, she had shed sixteen pounds in weight. She had been fed a liquid diet through a tube into her stomach and lost a lot of muscle mass. All her clothes didn't fit; most, including underwear, were baggy and loose fitting. She would have to start and build a whole new wardrobe.

During her time in hospital she had few visitors, including the Human Resource department of the police force. Two managers from her division came to see her on two occasions, once to learn the full extent of the damage to her body and a follow up visit to see if there were any roles within the police force. They explained that because of her injuries gained while working for the force, she would be financially secure, but her career within the force had come to an end. Chief Constable James Ingram visited. He had known Lucy Spires all her career. He made it clear she was no longer a police officer. He discreetly told her he had made it clear to every police department she was no longer an inspector and since her injuries from the accident meant she was now retired from the force. Therefore she could never be a threat to anyone. He also told her the crash was not an accident. The white van was stolen the day before and the driver was a known associate of Farooq El Haj. When the van was deliberately crashed into her car, the van's steering wheel airbag had activated and it had gone into the driver's face, breaking his nose. There was a trace of DNA in the blood residue. He then ran off. He was seen on CCTV getting into another stolen car and driven away at speed. The car was never traced. This also showed clear images of his face, so he was identified quite quickly. He was a known to be on the payroll of Farooq El Haj, a man called William Banks. The Chief Inspector went on to say he had disappeared, and that a large manhunt had yielded nothing. He believed he was at the bottom of the North-sea. Farooq El Haj wanted to make sure there were no loose ends and he wanted to make an example of this man.

Chief Constable James Ingram had put the case on hold. He had suspended any action until a new team could revaluate how to proceed. The work Lucy Spires had done was extremely useful and thorough. To bring Farooq El Haj to court and successfully prosecute would have to wait.

One of Lucy Spires' visitors was her new member of the team, DC Emma Harper. She had visited every few days, even when still in a coma. During that time, Lucy Spires learned from Emma Harper there had been a further two murders, both female sex workers, both killed in the same way. On their knees, both strangled, both had earrings pulled from dead ears. Both at retail parks around the early hours of the morning. Both had trophies taken after they were killed. No DNA was found to link any suspect. No witness statement yielded anything of any importance. Their 'Ghost' appeared, committed these awful crimes and vanished into the night. Both women discussed the case at length. Lucy Spires said he must have left a clue, must have some way to identify this murderer. DC Emma Harper told her they had exhausted all lines of enquiry, looking nationwide for any similar type of criminal activity.

Lucy Spires felt frustrated for the first time. She'd taken many positive steps since she became totally blind. She felt lucky to be alive; all she had lost was her sight. A massive thing to lose, but her determination to build a new life had kept her away from feelings of depression, or worse. She was given a blind cane with a small rubber ball on the end of it. She felt she would never get used to using this, but her independence depended on it. She went through in her mind every detail that DC Emma Harper had told her again and again about the murders, but she could not come up with an idea of who was committing these murders. But she knew there would be something, some tiny detail missed that would lead them to the person doing these crimes. As with the police policy, there had been a new Detective Chief Inspector appointed, Toby Butler, to take on the case. Emma Harper told her he didn't have the drive or enthusiasm she had. This made Lucy Spires feel a little better. Lucy Spires told Emma Harper the team must give him their support to catch this killer. She couldn't help herself, asking who was assigned to do what, how far the case had progressed, had they any suspects; too many questions for Emma Harper to answer. Lucy Spires felt a little hopeless. She wanted to help.

The day before her planned discharge, Chief Constable James Ingram visited. He wanted to make sure she felt safe going home and to fill her in on his decision to stop work on the Farooq El Haj case. He went on to explain the crash he felt was a deliberate act. He went on to say he felt Farooq El Haj must have known her plans so he tried to stop her. In other words, he felt she was betrayed by a member of her team. He urged her not to discuss any cases with anyone.

After a total of forty-four days, the hospital had a care package to release Lucy Spires. She was both looking forward to going home again, but a little scared at the thought of having to be an independent blind person. She knew it would be a gradual process to get used to living without sight. DC Emma Harper went to her home and brought a set of clothes to travel from the hospital to her home. All her clothes, including her underwear, still felt too big. She had gained a little weight as she had started to eat solid food.

Chief Constable James Ingram had arranged for DC Emma Harper to collect her from the hospital and take her home. She duly collected her and after feeling a little nervous in the car, arrived at her home. There was little conversation as Lucy Spires felt a little queasy. Entering her own front door and the smell of her home was a feeling she could never explain. Within an hour, coffee made with DC Emma Harper's help, all mail had been sorted. Luckily, all major issues had been sorted on her behalf by the Human Resources department from the police force. Lucy Spires felt comfortable with DC Emma Harper. She felt she could trust her as she was the newest member of her team and Lucy Spires felt she was a younger version of herself. She then didn't realise just how good friends they would become.

The carer met her at her front door, made her a light snack of a sandwich and muffin. She managed to eat them slowly as she still had a very poor appetite. The carer then ran her a hot bath. Lucy Spires added a lot more water. The carer explained she had to be very careful; if she slipped and banged her head and fell into the water, she could drown. Lucy Spires had a bath every night in that same house all her life. She knew every inch of her house. She asked the carer to leave as she was about to go in her bubbly, sweet smelling bath. The carer reluctantly left. Lucy Spires sank into her favourite place. She had so looked forward to this, but soon realised she had begun to cry, tears running down her face, a little cough started the outpour of emotions. She was a very private person and she kept her emotions in check. She remembered her mother saying she should have been an actress! The stress of the last weeks all came out and she cried out loudly. Screaming profanities at this uncalled act of sheer cowardice, her whole life had changed totally forever. But the saddest feeling she had was of being alone. Being alone to face her life as a blind, single woman. With her position in the police force, a large team to keep her mind busy, high level cases to solve and manage, goals to achieve in her life, all taken from her.

She emptied her bath water completely before she got out. Her soft warm, sweet smelling towels made her feel a little better. She went into her kitchen, found her wine bottles, reached into a cupboard for a wine glass, poured it and sipped it. It tasted so good, even though made her feel a little queasy. She stood and finished the glass; then she felt her way onto her sofa. She felt very tired. What the future held for her she couldn't even imagine. *Tomorrow is another day* she thought as she leaned into a cushion on the arm of her sofa. A short time later, she was in a restful sleep.

Chapter 5

Two weeks later, Lucy Spires had fallen into her routine. Her alarm went off at seven thirty. She managed to shower, dress herself, make coffee and make her own toast. She had a carer, coming to her at eight forty-five, to make sure she had breakfast and was set for the day. She now listened more to the radio as the television was not needed. A further carer visited at one o'clock, followed by a final carer at around seven thirty at night. She went to bed around ten thirty. She had realised, in her new of total blackness, it was a struggle to keep her mind from feeling it was permanent night time. She also felt that losing her sense of sight had meant her other senses had become sharper. When she listened to conversations, she would hear the words, but because there were no facial movements or body language, she found she listened in a new way. Time passed slowly. Days seemed to drag. Lucy Spires felt she needed a new challenge. Her confidence had grown and she was becoming the independent person she used to be.

Her favourite time was spent in her garden. She loved the warmth of the sun on her face, and each day she began to feel she had been both very lucky to survive the accident, but unlucky to have lost her sight. DC Emma Harper called regularly. She was living with a member of the fire service. He worked shifts and was a fitness fanatic, so he spent a lot of time at his gym maintaining a high level of fitness as needed in his work. Lucy Spires enjoyed her company as she gave updates of cases for Lucy Spires to deliberate over. She also brought updates on the team members. DC Phil Henderson had a new girlfriend; she was almost eight years younger. They both laughed as he was not blessed with good looks, but a fantastic personality, a funny man and an excellent detective. DC David Evans, a genial Welshman, a great husband, great family man, always trying to win the lottery, would waste most of it on holidays, loved the police force, but would retire if he had the funds and spend all his time with his children. DC Emma Harper said to Lucy Spires he was the clumsiest man she had ever met. He'd fallen out of his car and got a black eye. Fallen off a ladder trying to change his outdoor security light and had bruised his back, but his pride hurt more! They went on to discuss the other members of the team. All sent best wishes on her recovery.

DC Emma Harper called the following Wednesday. She brought her usual treat; this week it was cream cakes. Once they'd sat down with coffees, Lucy Spires was surprised to hear DC Emma Harper sound genuinely excited. She went on to discuss the outcome of a meeting with Chief Constable James Ingram. He had called DC Emma Harper into his office to discuss Lucy Spires as he knew they were in regular contact. He was frustrated the sex worker's murderer had not been caught, nor was the current Detective Chief Inspector, Toby Butler, any closer to bringing this man to justice. He wanted to use Lucy Spires' experience to help to solve this case. He wanted her to be 'an advisor' to the help solve the case. He felt a fresh outlook, with an open mind to re-look at intricate details, would bring massive benefits.

Lucy Spires' heart skipped a beat. DC Emma Harper had updated Lucy Spires with aspects of the case, but Chief Constable James Ingram actually wanted the help of Lucy Spires. DC Emma Harper went on to explain the details of her working for him. Lucy Spires would not be paid. She would have any expenses paid and any work done would be on a voluntary basis. Lucy Spires was speechless. She had too many questions buzzing around her head. Who would she report to? What resources could she use? How on earth could she assist on a complicated case such as this without her sense of sight?

For the first time in her memory, DC Emma Harper sat in silence as Lucy Spires digested the conversation they just had.

Both didn't speak for what felt like five minutes. DC Emma Harper spoke first. "I don't think our Chief Constable meant to upset you. I think he meant this as a huge compliment and you would bring a lot to this case."

Lucy Spires didn't know where to begin. Of course she wanted this chance to help. This was the fresh challenge she felt she needed. After a few moments, the other side to this began to unravel. Lucy Spires would need a new wardrobe. She had lost a great deal of weight, her hair was now growing back, but was still very short though the scars on her head had faded greatly.

Within an hour, the two women had ordered online new appropriate clothes, had arranged an appointment to give Lucy Spires a new makeover, new hairstyle, manicure, facials and a re-launch of her career as a police advisor. Lucy Spires rang the Chief Constable to arrange a date for a visit to the police headquarters and reconnect with her old team and get up to speed with this case. She knew this would be difficult as this could bring back the trauma of her life changing accident. Lucy Spires knew she had to move forward with her life.

The following day, DC Emma Harper collected Lucy Spires at nine-thirty, as arranged. First point of call, the hairdresser. After a quite brief discussion about hairstyles and colours, the stylist set to work to give Lucy Spires a modern look. Lucy Spires felt a little sad. She had always taken great pride in her appearance; hair, make up and all her clothes. After many compliments on her new hairstyle and colour, she was moved to a seat to begin her hands' makeover. She was placed on a chair with a towel under her hands. A young sounding stylist asked what colour she would like on her nails, if she was going on a date, or on holiday to Spain. This made Lucy Spires smile and asked for a subtle shade of pink as she was going back to work in a few days. As she told the young stylist this information, she felt a great deal of pride. DC Emma Harper took hold of her hands and looked at the finished nails.

"You look a million dollars, as my mum would say," said DC Emma Harper. "Lucy," she said. "I don't know how to say this, but have you considered wearing dark glasses, or have you any sunglasses?"

Lucy Spires was speechless. This was possibly a question she would never consider. She realised this was a difficult question her friend Emma had asked her.

"Emma," said Lucy Spires. "I hadn't even thought of that. If you think I should, then I'll need you to pick some for me as they were in my wrecked car and I didn't get them back."

There was a little pause, then DC Emma Harper spoke softly, "Lucy, since your accident, your eyes are a little different. One is a little red and the other is like a fixed stare." There was no other easy way to tell her. Lucy Spires, inhaled deeply and nodded in her direction.

"Emma," said Lucy Spires. "You should have told me. I never gave a second's thought to…" her voice trailed off.

"I'll sort out a good designer pair, modern sunglasses," said Emma Harper.

Lucy Spires smiled towards her friend and nodded. "Nothing too outrageous. Let me know how much and I'll sort it," said Lucy Spires.

"Will do," came her reply.

The following days, all of Lucy Spires' new wardrobe of clothes and shoes were delivered to the home of DC Emma Harper. She brought them to Lucy Spires. This seemed to give her more confidence, making her feel ready to take on the new challenge. She felt a little uneasy at the thought of catching up with her old team and a little worried at how Detective Chief Inspector Toby Butler would feel about the Chief Constable bringing in an advisor. But there had now been six brutally murdered women, and with no suspects and no positive leads, the case had stalled. The Chief Constable had to be seen to be doing something as he was under pressure.

Chapter 6

17th May

At six-thirty, Lucy Spires alarm sounded, although she was barely asleep. This was to be her first day back in police headquarters. She'd met Detective Chief Inspector Toby Butler on several occasions. She had a good opinion of him; he was diligent, courteous, polite and thorough in his methods. He'd had a very good crime success rate. He also didn't suffer fools. If you were not a team player, he didn't want you on his team. He led by example. He often worked eighteen-hour days and wouldn't ask any officer to do anything he hadn't done or wouldn't do himself.

As she prepared herself to be picked up at eight o-clock, a flutter of nerves gripped her. She steadied herself as she got into DC Emma Harper's car. The drive in the early sunshine was pleasant, the music on the radio never seeming to change. As they reached police headquarters, familiar things started as they pulled into the car park. There were two sets of speed humps and Lucy Spires thought how many times she had driven over them; it must number in the thousands. DC Emma Harper opened the door for Lucy Spires. A deep breath taken, she exited the car, held gently but firmly DC Emma Harper's arm and heard the click of her heels as she walked toward the building. She imagined a few lines of people at windows, wanting to have a look at the returning member. Lucy Spires walked in upright and as confident as possible. The two women paused at the front door as DC Emma Harper leant forward to press her electronic entry badge at the entry point. The door swung open with still the same creak as Lucy Spires remembered. The stairs had the same smell, a light dusty smell. Three flights later, DC Emma Harper opened the door for Lucy Spires, the noise of her heels disappearing on the carpeted floor. This was the top floor of police headquarters. Lucy Spires realised they weren't going to see the team of detectives, but instead to the office of Chief Constable James Ingram.

A polite knock on his door and both women entered. His office was very warm, with a faint smell of a familiar aftershave. DC Emma Harper guided them to seats opposite Chief Constable James Ingram. Lucy Spires felt a little nervous. She had tremendous respect for her Chief Constable, a tall, good looking man who cared with the same passion and commitment she always had.

"DC Harper," he said, "I really appreciate your help to get Lucy to this point."

Lucy Spires always felt he talked like a politician. He always said things in a roundabout way. She just liked to cut to the chase and say what had to be said.

"Lucy, you look great. I was a little worried in case you felt you weren't up to helping your colleagues on this case." he said in a matter of fact diction. Lucy Spires shuffled a little in her chair. He was usually very good at putting you at ease. "Lucy," he said, "I've had a long chat with DCI Toby Butler. His team have hit a brick wall. We need to catch this man and put him away for a very long time. I've assigned DC Emma Harper to work with you. I realise it may take a little time to get back up to speed on the aspects of the case as there have been developments."

Lucy Spires realised she was sat bolt upright. She felt her muscles were very tense. The Chief Constable moved from his chair. Lucy Spires followed his movements by the sound of his clothes. She heard the clink of cups. He was making coffee for them. A buzz came from a machine to her left.

"A latte with no sugar Lucy?" asked the Chief Constable.

"Oh, yes please," came her reply.

"Same for you DC Harper?" he said.

With a little croak in her voice, "Yes please Sir," said DC Emma Harper.

Chief Constable James Ingram gently placed Lucy Spires hand around the side of her cup. She could smell the fresh aroma of coffee. It was a surprise. Every meeting she had previously in his office, she had never been offered a beverage. A further discussion on the way forward, bringing this case to a close went on for a further twenty minutes. Chief Constable James Ingram asked DC Emma Harper to give them five minutes alone. She duly put down her cup and left the room.

"Lucy, I have no idea how difficult you will find this, but I have complete faith in you. I know you, and you will follow your instincts and bring this case to a close. As far as the Farooq El Haj case, it's ongoing. We will catch this slippery bastard. He isn't going anywhere. If you need my help on anything and I mean anything, my door is always open. I mean twenty-four hours every day." Following that he said it was time to meet the troops and get going.

After that, Chief Constable James Ingram took away both women's empty cups and gently took Lucy Spires' left hand, put it on his half folded left arm and they left his office, walking at a slow pace. He led them down one flight of stairs. Lucy Spires knew these well. Within a few seconds, the noise level increased as the three of them went through double wedged open doors.

As they came into the room, Lucy Spires could hear chairs move back, people standing up from their desks, phone calls and conversations cut short; a quietness descended. She heard a few quiet gasps as the team of police officers realised who she was. The Chief Constable paused near Detective Chief Inspector Toby Butler's office. He looked through the glass door, opened it and entered.

"Good morning Toby," said the Chief Constable. He rose to his feet. Lucy Spires could smell sweat in the air. The air was a little stale. She stood still while the detective came to her.

"Hi Lucy, how are you?" said the detective Chief Inspector.

"I'm ok," came her reply. She felt a little awkward. The last thing she wanted him to feel was threatened by her. She wanted his support and blessing to work with him and his team to bring in the murderer.

"Well, I'll leave our former DCI and DC Harper with you Toby. A fresh set of ideas may help. If you need me, let me know," said the Chief Constable.

Lucy Spires smiled a little; he always chose his words carefully. With that, his grip on her arm fell away and she felt a small blast of air on her face as the door to the office was opened and then closed as he left.

"Well, ladies," said Detective Chief Inspector Toby Butler. "Where to start. Lucy, most of the team you know, a few new faces. DC Harper will go through all the details we have. Six murders, no suspects, no evidence of sorts to move with. We have a ghost." He paused and handed DC Emma Harper a thick card file. Lucy Spires heard her say thank you. He looked in the direction of Lucy Spires. Her sunglasses made him feel a little uncomfortable. He felt he wasn't too happy with having to work with a now blind, ex-detective chief inspector, who he hoped in one way would solve these crimes, but at the same time hoped she would fail and he would have shown his doubters he was the man to succeed.

DC Harper stood up. "We'll get started straight away sir. Can we use the desk next to mine, near the window? It has a little bit more space than the work station," she said.

He looked up and gave a subtle shrug which she took to mean yes.

With that, she lifted Lucy Spires hand onto her arm and guided her to the door. It swung inward, knocking against Lucy Spires' foot. It didn't hurt, nor had anyone noticed. DC Emma Harper led her to her desk. Lucy Spires could sense the atmosphere was a little tense. She could sense a lot of eyes staring at her. This made her feel uncomfortable and question why she had agreed to do this. She felt a little wave of panic; her heart was beating faster than normal. She was lost for words and felt a little scared. She felt a brush of someone at her left side. There was a familiar smell, but she couldn't place it.

"Hello Ma'am, it's great to see you back," said detective David Evans. He continued, "We were all so worried about you, that accident couldn't have been any worse. We were told initially it was fatal! When we found you'd pulled through… Well, we were all relieved." This made her smile as she had always seen him as an excellent detective and a loyal, reliable friend. "Ma'am, I've never seen you with hair as short as that, it makes you look younger," said detective David Evans.

There was a small ripple of laughter, and this eased her feelings of tension. Lucy Spires stood up, and the room fell silent. She took a breath and said, "Guys, I was told, when I came out of my coma, of all your best wishes for my recovery. But can I just say I'm not an officer anymore, which includes a title. In other words, please call me Lucy. Our Chief Constable asked me to try and help bring this case to an end. I hate leaving loose ends and we really need to catch this guy. I'm going to need all your help and support, even more than before." The silence of everyone took her by surprise and a smile crept onto her face. A landline began to ring to her left and a little behind her. Another voice she knew well spoke, this time from further away.

"Ma'am, I mean Lucy, I'm just going to make a coffee. Can I get you your usual?" said Detective Phil Henderson.

"Phil" replied Lucy Spires, "I'd love one. If I'd known you'd be here I'd have brought them bloody awful fig rolls you like! How on earth you eat them is beyond me!"

She heard his chair move, his keys jingle on his belt hook. He always had a large bunch of keys and because of that his colleagues called him 'the jailer!' A few seconds later she felt him squeezing her shoulders; his big strong hands felt warm and a comfort. She had always liked him. He was a very diligent, observant officer who had a great deal of patience. He would look at things again and again until satisfied in his own mind he had gone down every route. She moved and touched his hand on her shoulder. This re-assured her she had done the right thing in coming back to help. He was one of the first officers to join her Major Investigation Team. He could have progressed within the force, but wanted to stay with Lucy Spires as he enjoyed working as part of her team. She had often heard him say every day was different and that there couldn't be a better job.

Over the next few hours, the other members of her old team made a point of catching up with Lucy Spires. This was the first day ever she had drunk so many cups of coffee. Lucy Spires also quickly realised DC Emma Harper was now a very good member of the team. Chief Inspector Toby Butler had been in his office all day. She knew the pressure he was under; he had this high-level case to work on as well as several more. As the day went on, DC Emma Harper and other detectives went through all the details of the unlawful deaths.

In total, six female sex workers had been strangled on various nights during the week. The home office pathologist had reported they were strangled and had been on their knees in front of the person who took their lives. There was evidence of sexual activity from all the women and some DNA evidence, but none showed up on any records to give a name. Hair samples were found, but again no match on any databases. There were fibres of what the pathologist felt were from leather gloves, the type worn doing manual work, gardening or building, and were very common. They could be bought from any DIY outlet, online or hardware shop. Every victim had had jewellery removed after death; earrings had been pulled out of ears and on one occasion a nose piercing had been removed, again after death occurred. The reports stated the strength to commit these unlawful killings was considerable. The pathologist went on to explain he virtually lifted their whole body off the ground with a lot of force to strangle them, and breaking the windpipe would take very strong hands and arms. All the murders were, in his opinion, committed by the same person. There were drugs, class A and class B, present in five out of six women. Lucy Spires felt a little sad. In her time in Vice she had come to realise no female of any age would prefer to do this as a profession. They did it either to feed a family, as in the case of Julie Ann Cooper, a single mother, trying to feed her daughter and support her mother, or to feed a serious drug habit. Some sex workers had tried to find help from drug agencies, but had fallen back into drug use, a vicious circle with no way out for them. At around four-fifteen, Chief Constable James Ingram appeared next to Lucy Spires. She noticed his aftershave as he neared her.

"Well Lucy, how was your first day?" he asked.

Lucy Spires swung around in her chair. Her left foot stopped against the Chief Constable's foot so she knew she was in front of him. She took a deep breath and said, "The team have been brilliant. We've gone through what little evidence we have. It's much the same as before my accident, but we need to think outside the box. There are other lines of enquiry we can look at. There must be things we can link together, there must be a pattern we haven't seen. I made a promise to myself after victim number four, Julie Ann Cooper, a single mother, lost her life, to find her killer. I would like to keep that commitment sir."

After she had finished speaking, Chief Constable James Ingram looked surprised. "Lucy," he said, "I knew you would take this on and give two hundred percent." Lucy spires felt his foot move. He had turned his body, looking toward DC Emma Harper. "Detective Harper," he said in his usual confident voice. "Please take Lucy home. I think this is enough for today." He turned back toward Lucy Spires and he spoke softly as he was very near her. "A very good first day back in the fold, but I think we need to take it slowly. I'm aware of all your injuries, the main one in front of me. I don't want to make you unwell." His voice changed as Toby Butler came out of his office. "Good progress, today. Lucy, as you are a volunteer, would you like to come back in tomorrow or the following day? DC Harper will coordinate collecting you and what you may need."

Lucy Spires moved her head back and replied she would like to return the same time the following day. He turned toward DC Harper. She said she would sort out the details with Lucy Spires on her drive to her home. He moved away from her desk toward Toby Butler. Lucy Spires heard the office door open. She imagined the two men entered for a de-brief.

Lucy Spires felt down by her feet for her handbag. She picked it up, pulled it around her right shoulder just as DC Emma Harper placed her hand on her left arm. They carefully made their way back to the car. Lucy Spires was deep in thought and didn't speak. DC Emma Harper opened the door for Lucy Spires. As she sat in the passenger seat, she felt very tired, ready to fall asleep. It was too early for that and she felt very hungry.

"Emma," said Lucy Spires, "I've had a great day, but I'm very hungry. Will you take me home via fast food fried chicken in a bucket. I need to fill my belly and try and come up with a strategy to bring closure to this case." The car veered to the right.

"That is a super idea, but as you know a bucket of crispy chicken is made for sharing!" Lucy smiled at the reply.

Less than hour later, a bucket full of chicken gone, along with several dips and fries, caffeine filled drinks gone, the two women started to discuss the case. Two hours later, DC Emma Harper was making her way home. Lucy Spires had a relaxing bath, then turned in to bed, feeling exhausted; but the little flutter of butterflies she felt as she pulled the bed sheets over her body meant she had the best kind of reasons to get out of her bed tomorrow.

Chapter 7

Lucy Spires was waiting with anticipation for DC Emma Harper to collect her at eight o'clock. The local radio was playing the same music as usual. The hourly news came on. Lucy Spires half listened. The same politicians were in the news, the same sports results, a quick weather update and as always, the problems with rush hour traffic. She just caught the end of the traffic report saying the roads around the Low Meadows Retail Park, in the north of the city, were closed due to a police incident. Her heart sank. She thought *please, please let this not be his next victim*. She knew the area well. An established area used by both male and female sex workers. This was the worst possible news if this was his latest victim. Many thoughts ran through her mind; a young single mother, a young vulnerable girl, a drug user or a combination of all three. She sat on the edge of her sofa. The emotions she felt were building. There was a knock on the front door. Lucy Spires reached the door in a few seconds and heard the voice of DC Emma Harper, saying it was her and that she had come to collect her.

In her car, in less than two minutes DC, Emma Harper updated her that it was indeed another unlawful killing. Initial indications pointed toward a copy of the previous victims. Chief Constable James Ingram had contacted DC Emma Harper directly; he wanted Lucy Spires involved immediately. He felt he needed every single person on this case. He went on to tell DC Emma Harper the pressure on everyone had just been ramped up. There had now been seven women who have lost their lives. He was determined that this will be his last. DC Emma Harper said he was very upset. She felt he had taken this personally. Lucy Spires felt unusual butterflies in her stomach. She was always a calm person, never suffering from nerves. She remembered the only time she had felt anxious was at the funeral of her mother, as she realised she would never see her again.

They arrived at police headquarters and moved through a group of reporters, who were already there waiting for the mandatory statement from a senior officer. In the past, Lucy Spires had been involved in some of these. She wouldn't miss any of it. They went straight to the Major Incident Room. As they entered the noise level was noticeably louder; phones were ringing, several conversations going on, the atmosphere felt very tense. Just as they sat at the same desk as before, Lucy Spires heard her old office door hinge make the familiar sound as it opened. Chief Detective Inspector Toby Butler came into the centre of the room. A silent wave came over the room.

"Guys, we've got a better picture of events from this morning," he said. Lucy Spires heard the team shuffling around. She guessed they were getting ready to make written notes as they would be allocated specific tasks to start once the briefing was over.

Toby Butler had their attention. Lucy Spires heard a click as he either took his spectacles off his head, or put them on; she couldn't remember him wearing them. He started, "At four this morning a twenty-three-year-old female, now identified as Lyndsay Marie Walker, was found at the rear of the Low Meadows Retail Park, by a supermarket delivery driver. He was turning his articulated vehicle around, ready to make an early delivery when he caught sight of the victim in his headlights. Initial indications are the same as the previous unlawful killings. We need to stop this from happening again. My budget has just been increased. I'm trying to get more officers to knock on doors." With that, he began giving specific tasks to his team. The only two not mentioned were DC Emma Harper and Lucy Spires. "Ladies," he said, "Can I have a word in my office?"

Lucy Spires was guided into his office. There was the same stale air as yesterday. She sat down on a leather seat; it made a squeak as she moved. "Lucy," he said, "how the hell are we going to get this murdering bastard?" His voice full of tension.

She crossed her legs and took a deep breath. She had been quiet for too long. She started, "Toby, knocking on doors will do nothing for this case apart from be a PR exercise. There must be a pattern, he has to have made a mistake. We have to re-visit every crime again. We need to look in detail at every post mortem, every bit of forensic evidence, plus I'm convinced CCTV will be the key. In all these retail parks there is face recognition CCTV, number plate ID recognition. There must be something we aren't seeing!" With that she moved again, the same sound came from the seat.

She heard Toby Butler sit on the opposite side of her. She heard a shuffle of papers on the desk and he lifted his landline phone. He pressed two buttons and she heard a faint ring.

"DC Booth," came a faint reply.

"Hi Marie, will you bring all the files from the following unlawful killings. Elizabeth Jane Peterson, Lyndsey Murray, Susan Carlin, Julie Ann Cooper, Paula Cassidy and Emma Little. Will you also please get two lattes for Emma Harper and Lucy Spires. They'll be using my office. I've an appointment with a home office pathologist then a press conference to prepare for. Please give them all the help they need. Please get them any information they may need. Cheers Marie." With that he stood up. "Emma, you two get your heads together. We need to move up a gear. As you said Lucy, we don't have time for a PR exercise. We need to get a name and we need to close this. Lucy, you know this team better than I do. Get them doing the things they do best." With that, she heard his chair move back, his jacket swung on. "Emma," he said. "Look after Lucy. Both of you go through these files, look at them with an open mind. If you're right Lucy, there must be things we've missed. Get me on my mobile. If I don't answer, I'll get back to you." With that the door swished open and closed after him.

Before the two women could even speak, the door opened again. It was DC Marie Booth carrying an arm full of files. She placed them on the desk and halved the files.

"Oh," said DC Marie Booth. "Do you take sugar?" she asked a little nervously.

"No," came the joint reply.

With that she turned and left the office. DC Emma Harper stood up and picked up a file. "We'll start with them in order. Elizabeth Jane Peterson. Unlawfully killed February thirteenth, person/persons unknown." She sat next to Lucy Spires, had a drink of her coffee and passed the other cup to her friend.

"Emma, we don't need to go through these files. I wrote most of them! Please look at the back of the files for updated notes, dated after my accident. Look for new witness statements, or anything that will help," she said.

She heard the turning of pages and DC Emma Harper pause for a few seconds, reading dates, reading them through. Lucy Spires felt a little frustrated. She thought *give me back my eyes, just for a few days*. DC Emma Harper brought her out of her daydream.

"The only thing I can see is a report of a black or dark coloured quiet motorbike, no lights, no crash helmet and no registration number plate, seen by the witness who discovered our victim." Lucy Spires had heard this before. She seemed to remember a report of a motorbike seen at the crime scene.

Two hours later, they had gone through all the crime files and had identified a further line of enquiry. A motorbike now meant a means of how the murderer got to the scene of the crime and left. With that information, DC Emma Harper tried to ring Detective Chief Inspector Butler to tell him of this albeit minor breakthrough and see how he wanted to move forward. There was no answer from his mobile. Lucy Spires decided to take the initiative and she asked DC Emma Harper to take her to DC Phil Henderson. She had a very important job for him. They came out of the Chief Detective's office and found there was a hush around the room. She was guided to his desk. He turned and stood up as she began to talk.

"Phil," said Lucy Spires, "we've got a task for you. We've identified how our offender got to and from the crime scenes. The issue is a little complicated. Our offender used a black or dark coloured motorcycle to commit these crimes. But because of the geography and distance between the assaults, I think he had another vehicle used to transport this motorcycle nearby, then change to commit the offence, and then back to the vehicle. Where the offences took place, to use a motorcycle with no lights, no crash helmet and missing a registration number would show up on CCTV nearby. Phil, you've always had a sharp eye for detail. I need you to find where this bike came from, where it went to and get this man behind bars. Look at every evening before the murders. The retail parks have superb cameras, they must show us some detail. Once we have this then we should go knocking on doors." With that, the buzz around the room resumed.

DC Emma Harper was a little in awe of Lucy Spires. Her way of thinking once explained made perfect logic. Lucy Spires felt a little tired; she had been concentrating for several hours now. Both women went back into the Chief Detective's office and Lucy Spires told Emma Harper she was tired. They had been concentrating for several hours.

Just over an hour later, DC Phil Henderson burst into the office. It made Lucy Spires jump. "Ma'am, sorry, Lucy," he said. "I think I've found a link. But it's not a bloody black motorbike! I found a few images of a motor bike, no distinguishing features possible as all images were taken at night, plus random directions away from the crime scenes." He paused to clear his throat. Lucy Spires could feel her heart rate increase. *Get to point* she heard herself say in a very impatient voice. "Well, Miss Spires!" said Phil Henderson. "I decided to look at vehicles going into the retail parks or around the area big enough to hide a cycle, I thought of a larger vehicle, a van, a lorry, a large 4X4. And the only vehicle in the area on four occasions was a single seven and a half tonne, bright blue lorry, with a large logo of 'Shopwell Tyres' emblazoned on the side. Plus I checked CCTV from yesterday and yes, there it was again at Low Meadows Retail

Park. At the back of all the parks are various tyre and exhaust repair centres, some independent businesses or part of a national chain. It stuck out in my mind as my daughter texted me yesterday that she needs two new tyres before her car has an MOT." With that he took a long breath and said, "Lucy, it's great to have you back!"

Lucy Spires' heart was pounding. The noise volume in the incident room increased. Usually in her role in charge she would be allocating jobs to her team. She took a breath. "Phil, I could kiss you!" she said. "Emma, please get a hold of Toby Butler. We need to update him. He should be finished at the hospital," said Lucy Spires. She shuddered at the thought of the last time she had been to the post mortem of Julie Ann Cooper and what happened a minute later. DC Emma Harper passed a phone to Lucy Spires. They talked for fifteen minutes, going through the breakthrough they'd found. He said to wait until he returned to headquarters as he would have to discuss this with Chief Constable James Ingram. They would have to be careful and see this carefully to its conclusion. He said he was on his way. Lucy Spires asked the team to find out all they could about the company called 'Shopwell Tyres'. Check to see if there were tyre and exhaust centres at all of the other retail parks where offences had occurred, plus any other information they could get for her prior to seeing Chief Constable James Ingram.

Thirty minutes later, Detective Chief Inspector Toby Butler was filling in the details of the morning autopsy. He had come straight from the Queen Ann Hospital. The victim a twenty-two-year-old sex worker, brutally killed in the same way as the other girls. Twenty minutes later, detective chief inspector held Lucy Spires arm as they went into the Chief Constable James Ingram's office. He gestured them to take a seat.

"Well done Lucy," he said. "I knew you would bring things to this case." With that he moved over to her, he gently squeezed her shoulder and he continued, "Toby, where do we go from here? Do we have any other evidence apart from the work the team has done today on this tyre company, what is its name?" He flicked a page over on his desk. "Yes, Shopwell Tyres. What else do we know about this company or the employees?" He sat down waiting for the reply.

Toby Butler wasn't too keen on his Chief Constable. He liked the praise when things were going well and figures showed crime rates down and he was aligned with his financial budgets. Detective Chief Inspector Toby Butler sat upright in his chair. He had given this new evidence some thought. "Well Sir, we only have visual evidence this lorry was in the area. No other evidence to give a name, or even prove the driver of this vehicle is the same man. We don't have any viable reason to even ask for a search warrant to go after anyone in the company." He got out a notebook. His team had done some research on the company. "Sir, the company is an importer of all makes and brands of tyres. It's a family run company and they have been in business for twenty years. They supply daily deliveries across the North of England to any company needing tyres. They employ around fifty people. Shopwell Tyres also own nine garages fitting tyres and exhausts." The Chief Constable held up his hand and the detective went silent.

"Lucy," said the Chief Constable. "How sure are you this new evidence will prove fruitful?"

Lucy Spires took a long breath. "This is our only lead. There are no such things as coincidences. We have the vehicle on CCTV at the retail parks the day before each murder. Right time, right place," she said.

"I agree," said the Chief Constable. "I thought we were looking for a black motor bike? This means we have another line of enquiry. Good progress."

With that, they knew it was time to leave the Chief Constable to it. Lucy was guided back to the main office where DC Emma Harper was waiting for her.

"Time to take you home," said DC Emma Harper, "It's been a long but productive day. Who knows what will happen tomorrow!"

With that, Lucy Spires asked DC Emma Harper to get her handbag as she was ready to go home. An hour later, Lucy

Spires had eaten her meal, her carer had called to cook her dinner, and made sure she was settled and left. As Lucy Spires settled down with a relaxing glass of wine, her phone began to ring. Only a few people had her number.

"Hi Lucy. Great Day!" It was Chief Constable James Ingram. He went on, "I've spoken to the Crime Prosecution Service. They won't give any warrant to look closer at this 'Shopwell Tyres' company. But I have a little idea to get them to help us, discreetly of course. Will you come to my office when you get to HQ tomorrow?" He had a way of making you want to help.

"I'll ask DC Harper to bring me up to your office when I arrive. Your coffee is nicer than the coffee in the office canteen," said Lucy Spires. She heard a little laugh.

"Miss Spires, you drive a hard bargain. Have a nice evening. See you tomorrow." With that he terminated the call.

What he had in mind, Lucy Spires had no clue.

Chapter 8

DC Emma Harper collected Lucy Spires at eight o'clock the next day. It was a warm, bright, sunny morning. On the journey to Police Headquarters, Lucy Spires told her friend about the phone call the previous evening. Lucy said she'd slept badly because of the anticipation of the Chief Constable's cryptic call. She needed a strong latte to kick start her day. DC Emma Harper called at a new coffee drive through for cups of kick start double shot coffee and Danish pastries. A slow drive later and they arrived ready for a busy, full day.

They went straight to the office of the Chief Constable. He met them at the door carrying a box with a new mobile phone in his hand. He smiled at DC Emma Harper and Lucy Spires.

"Good morning. A beautiful sunny day and the latest hi-tech phone has finally arrived," he said with a wide smile. "Have a seat while, as promised, I'm your coffee maker for this morning." Lucy Spires had forgotten the last piece of the evening conversation.

"Two nice and strong fresh Lattes?" he said.

"Yes please," said Lucy Spires before DC Emma Harper could even draw a breath.

"Well, after I spoke to the department to look at trying to get a warrant to look more closely at 'Shopwell Tyres', I thought of a way to get them on our side." With that he gave them their coffees.

Lucy Spires heard him move to behind his desk. He coughed a little to clear his throat. She could hear him tapping numbers on his desk telephone. She could hear a faint ringing tone and then she heard a female voice answer. "Good morning, can I speak to the managing director please?" he said with his usual confidence. Lucy Spires thought he would have made a very good politician. He had confidence and was always very sure of himself. A few seconds later, the soft female voice asked who was calling. "Oh, my name is Chief Constable James Ingram. I would like to discuss our fleet of ninety-two vehicles. I think most may need new tyres." She put him straight through. He looked at DC Emma Harper and smiled. "Ah, yes good morning Mr Richardson. My name is James Ingram, Chief Constable for the Northern Constabulary. Our tender for our tyres is due for review for our fleet of ninety-two vehicles. I wouldn't usually get involved personally, but I have to keep a very close eye on budgets. Your company was mentioned at the last charity function I was asked to attend and again at my golf club. As you can imagine, we use a lot of vehicles every day of the year and need to maintain them in top condition. I'll have my garage manager email the sizes and types we use. If you can get that back to me, my team will make a decision very quickly." He again smiled in the direction of DC Emma Harper, who, by this time, had drunk her strong coffee. She looked at Lucy Spires; the cup in her hand was also empty. A few seconds later and the conversation was over.

The Chief Constable went on to explain his plan to get 'Shopwell Tyres' to help with their investigations. He also felt the sightings of a black motor cycle in the area was a pure coincidence. He wanted the main focus to be the tyre company. Both women left the office impressed with his proactive, unusual approach. He was to ring the managing director back in a few hours and use his charm and potential business dealings to open any door needed to complete their investigations.

Three hours later, detective chief inspector Toby Butler called DC Emma Harper and Lucy Spires into his office. "Sit down ladies, you've charmed our Chief Constable into doing some police work. We have unofficial access to 'Shopwell Tyres'. Apparently the MD shares the same golf club. He will be at his office after the rest of the staff have gone home to assist with our enquiries. Tonight is overtime for you DC Harper, along with DC Henderson and DC Evans. Travel in one car. Lucy, you can go with them or get dropped off at home."

Lucy Spires said she would like to go with them if possible. At six-fifteen, the four set off to the biggest depot of Shopwell Tyres and the head office of the company.

When they arrived at the depot a short time later, they were met by the managing director Jack Richardson and his son William. The two men greeted them under a large 'Reception' sign. Inside the office, the two owners offered the team coffee or tea, but they declined. The team were really interested in one of the large lorries used on the specific dates. They had the registration number of the vehicle. The team didn't examine any vehicles. The brief they were given was to obtain information of potential suspects, the drivers of the vehicles, but keep the investigation low key, with the reason for the investigation to routinely dismiss the vehicles from their enquiries.

To make sure the two owners weren't aware of the real reason for the investigations, they took the details of all the vehicles and acquired, more importantly, names of all the drivers. In particular, the main suspect, now known as 'Richard Edward Garner'. The managing Director said all his drivers usually drove the same vehicles on the same routes. The only exceptions were the companies requiring early deliveries or very late deliveries. This was the main reason for an overnight stay. He went on and said that the lorries had a lot of deliveries across the Northern region, even delivering tractor tyres to farms. The son of the managing director told Lucy Spires they all had 'nicknames'. Richard Edward Garner was also known as 'Hairless Reg'. His initials were his nickname. He was called "Hairless Reg as he shaved his entire body hair off! The son of the managing director told Lucy Spires he had worked for his company for around ten years. He lived alone and was a reliable, loyal employee. He was even known to take his lorry home at weekends to clean and polish it. He went on to say that his neighbours thought he was a lovely man. He helped elderly neighbours keep their gardens tidy and did a lot of shopping for them. He never took holidays. He didn't mind staying out over night as he had no reason to rush home. He was, in the managing director's opinion, his best worker. The team learned he was scheduled to be away overnight the next three Wednesday nights. They took details of all other employees to make sure no-one was missed as a potential suspect. Lucy Spires took the initiative and asked both men not to tell any members of staff of the police investigation. Her reasons were the police were often seen wasting resources and their time. The managing director said he had no intention of informing them of the police activity; after all, it was routine enquiries to eliminate his employees from serious crimes committed and his company possibly obtaining a lucrative contract.

DC Emma Harper took Lucy home. She felt both exhausted and excited. There was now a named suspect, a serious person of interest. She knew the next day, the team would be tasked to find out everything about this man. She looked forward to the following day with anticipation. A few hours later, as she lay in bed, she felt her life had new meaning and a purpose. Her mind went back to the Farooq El Haj case. She would have liked to bring that particular case to a successful close. He was a particularly vicious and dangerous man. She wondered how his girlfriend was; the information passed by her had been vital. Lucy Spires wondered how many lives he had devastated by bringing in more drugs, people trafficked into the country and all the other illegal crimes he was involved in. She wondered who within the police force was informing Farooq El Haj of the police investigations and keeping him one step ahead of arresting him. Before her mind started on a course of going through details of the case, she knew she needed to sleep. She knew that would have to wait for another day.

Eight o'clock came around and DC Emma harper duly collected her friend. Lucy Spires noticed a different smell as she got into the car.

"Emma," said Lucy as they drove away. "New perfume? Smells nice!"

"Not really," came the reply "I've ran out of my usual one. My fella got me this one for my birthday. I'm not too keen as it reminds me of his mother, so I haven't got a lot on! Still, got to keep him happy!" A little laugh came as she said that.

As they drove to police headquarters, they went through the previous day's successful outcome. Lucy Spires felt DC Emma Harper was learning a lot from this case and would long term be an excellent detective, although she all too often talked about her now long-term boyfriend and how she would love to marry him and have several children. Lucy Spires thought about her marriage and how she was committed to detective work. She realised in her youth, DC Emma Harper should enjoy her life, as when she got older things would change for her.

The two women went into the main Major Crime office. Detective Chief Inspector Toby Butler was in his office and gestured to DC Emma Harper to come into his office. They came in and closed the door.

"Well ladies," he started. "Last night was a result. The intel on Richard Edward Garner is coming in." Lucy Spires heard a rustle of paper. "Brought up by his mother, an only child, she passed away when the young Garner was sixteen years old. Interestingly no name given on his birth certificate for his father. Unmarried he lived in several council rented properties as he grew up, went to several schools, was an average student, has worked as a driver for a few companies. This is the longest time in his current job, and he has no criminal record. Never been on our radar. Has a small amount of money in his bank, one credit card with an outstanding forty-pound debt. Has lived in the same rented council house for the last six years, with his rent paid up to date. The CPS are a bit reluctant to go further as we have no other evidence to go on."

He went on, "If he is our killer, we have a duty to stop him. I've got a team on him now. He's under observation twenty-four hours. I've been given the okay to do whatever it takes to catch this man. I just worry in case we've got the wrong man and we use up resources badly." He paused. Lucy heard him take a drink; she could smell coffee.

"Toby," said Lucy Spires. "We have nothing else to go on, we might as well give this our attention. Plus, I know we have something here. Watching this man will not break our bank and as you said, we have a duty to catch this killer. Sooner or later, we will have the proof." Lucy Spires left it there.

Chapter 9

The following week, the surveillance team had very little to report. Monday and Tuesday, the person of interest Richard Edward Garner started work at six-thirty am and delivered tyres all over the North and got back to the 'Shopwells Tyre' depot around 4 pm both days. On Wednesday, he started at 10 am as he would stay overnight for early deliveries the following day. They followed his lorry through the deliveries he made during the day. He eventually ended his driving at a main motorway services lorry park for the night. The team tailing him watched his lorry all through the night. He only left the vehicle twice, once at seven pm to have a bite to eat, then just after midnight he went for a shower. The team checked his lorry every few hours. They could hear music and a light was on in his cab part of the lorry, although they couldn't see inside as it was too high.

Meanwhile, at midnight, around six miles away, behind an established retail park, a small, blond woman watched as a dark motorcycle pulled near her and stopped. A man wearing leather trousers and jacket pulled it onto its stand. He slowly walked over and she half smiled. He had been several times to her in the last few months. She knew what he liked. As he neared, she saw the familiar way his leather trousers seemed to become loose around his waist. He stopped walking, so she took a few more steps toward him. Within a few seconds, he put on his condom. She knelt in front of him and he pushed his erect condom covered penis into her mouth. She rocked her head forward and back and she squeezed her jaws gently together. The sooner this was over, the better.

A few seconds later, she felt his body shudder as he climaxed. He had his gloved hands gently on the sides of her head. In a seamless movement, he moved his hands to the front of her neck. In an instant he was holding her in a grip she couldn't move away from. The grip was so strong she could feel she was almost lifted off the cold ground. She passed out in a very short time. Death followed soon after. The same routine was followed; trousers carefully pulled back up, condom still on his erect penis, careful to leave no trace of any fluids, nothing to point to her killer. She was moved and placed on her knees. Trophy earrings were taken. A last look at this woman; *one less prostitute was on this earth*, he thought as he mounted his motorcycle. He silently slipped away. He didn't start the engine until he was some distance away. He was a ghost, a shadow. He would never be caught as he was too clever. He had the power of life and death in his hands. He had done his research for the last few years. He had removed scum from this earth. He had started on his mission and would never stop until they were all gone.

The following morning, he left the motorway services at just a few minutes after six am. He completed his first delivery at six-fort-five, then through to his last delivery around three-thirty pm then back to the depot. The following week followed the same pattern. Luckily, no-one was found unlawfully killed.

The following week started as the week before. Monday, a usual day; Tuesday, the same. Wednesday, the same start as the week before; he started work around 10am, the lorry laden with stock to be delivered. The pattern was a similar one to the previous week. Late afternoon, he again parked his lorry in a different motorway service station, at the far end of the lorry park. The two plain-clothed detectives were parked in the car area. They parked so they could see if the suspect lorry moved. They observed the driver going for a meal around six, returning to his vehicle a half an hour later. He remained there until he went for a shower at one am. Both undercover officers thought this a strange time and followed him into the motorway service area. He asked the attendant in the retail shop for the key to the shower room.

Strangely, he asked the attendant, "Do you have an idea of the time?"

The young foreign attendant said it was one twenty-five am and pointed to a clock on a wall above and behind him. He went into the shower; about twenty-five minutes later, he was seen walking back to his lorry. The two undercover officers saw him enter his lorry. He didn't leave until six am. They began to follow him on his deliveries, a normal start to the day.

At seven forty-five, Lucy Spires was sitting, ready to be collected by DC Emma Harper when her phone began to ring. "Lucy." It was Detective Chief Inspector Toby Butler. "I'm afraid we've been looking at the wrong man. There was another crime last night. Another woman unlawfully killed. The same way. Initial reports suggest the same as all the others. I haven't been able to contact our Chief Constable to update him. He won't be happy." Lucy Spires' heart sank.

"Toby," she said. "Where did this happen? Do we have a time of death?"

"It's Ward Valley Retail Park, and preliminary time of death is between midnight and one am. A female, mid-twenties. Forensics said they found the victim kneeling in a similar position as previous victims, earrings taken post mortem. Looks like we're back to square bloody one!" came the reply.

Lucy Spires was lost for words. Toby Butler ended the call. A knock on her door brought her back to her senses. She opened it to hear the familiar voice of DC Emma Harper.

"On my way here. Butler rang me with the news. He said he was going to ring you after me," said DC Emma Harper.

"Yes, I've just taken his call. Emma I was sure we had the right man. His profile fitted, the timing of him in the area fits. Too many right things for it not to be this man."

The two women set off for police headquarters. Lucy Spires' brain was working overtime. When they arrived at police headquarters, just going over the familiar speed humps entering the car park, Lucy Spires asked DC Emma Harper to stop as soon as she could. She needed a minute to go through

71

things in her mind. The car came to a slow stop. DC Emma Harper didn't say a word and tried to breathe quietly.

After a minute of silence, DC Emma Harper took a short, sharp breath and said, "Lucy, we have a briefing with DCI Butler in less than ten minutes. We can't be late for that or I'll be back on foot patrol." With that she opened her door, went to the other side of the car and helped Lucy Spires out and toward the building. Lucy Spires' head was still spinning.

There were a lot of voices Lucy Spires could hear as they neared the meeting room. Too many voices to pick up an individual conversation. As the two women entered the room, Chief Constable James Ingram strode in just after them. Lucy Spires could tell it was him by his aftershave. He moved to the front of the room, standing next to detective Chief Inspector Toby Butler. It was the Chief Inspector who spoke.

"Team, we now have what appears to be our eighth unlawful killing. Our latest victim's identity is still to be confirmed. No finger print info. I guess there is no police record. No ID on our victim either. She's been taken to Queen Ann's hospital for a PM later today. It looks like our only suspect is not our killer. The team trailing him, DC Vicki Wallace and DC David Evans, sat with the lorry all last night. Our man had a bite to eat around six, then went for a shower at one am. His vehicle was parked up and remained there all night. We have to start again. We identified one suspect, we need to re-apply ourselves and find this offender before he does it again!"

Chief Constable James Ingram coughed to clear his throat and spoke quite calmly and quietly. "I know this has been a difficult case, with leads hard to dig up. I, as well as you all did a few weeks ago, thought we had our man. He fitted what we were looking for, right place, right dates. I personally never believe in coincidences. I look for facts, facts that cannot be questioned in any court. I need every member of this team to look at every detail again and again to find me this cowardly killer and bring a guilty verdict from a high court judge. Leave no stone unturned. DCI Butler and I are open to any ideas you may have, any avenues we should go down. I really feel we have a super team who will bring this case to book. I'll leave it there. My door is always open." With that he nodded at Detective Chief Inspector Toby Butler to follow him. They left to discuss this further in his office, one floor above.

Lucy Spires was shown to her usual desk. She could feel the sunshine through the window She didn't realise she was tapping her pen on her desk. Gradually voices faded away at the constant beat of pen on wood and the room became very quiet. Lucy Spires was going through details in her head repeatedly. DC Phil Henderson walked over to her and gently held her tapping hand, so she would stop. She knew it was DC Phil Henderson as he had his own unique smell.

"Lucy," he said, "what's going through your mind?"

Lucy Spires moved in her chair. Her posture was very straight. "Guys, I still feel our lorry driver, Richard Edward Garner, is our man. The leg work, the dates, the timing, are too coincidental to be anyone else." She paused for a few seconds. "Are Vicki Wallace or David Evans here?" she asked. DC Phil Henderson answered they had worked the nightshift, so had gone home to catch a few hours' sleep. Both would be into work early this afternoon.

During the next few hours, Lucy Spires sat quietly, trying to work out what she had missed. Had she really wanted it to be this Tyre delivery driver? Dismissing any other evidence along the way which would have meant a poor woman would still be alive today. A warm coffee was placed in her hand, the first for over two hours. DC Emma Harper had got some food from headquarters canteen; it was a cold tasteless sandwich. Lucy Spires hadn't realised she hadn't eaten for several hours. After forcing the food down, a not too familiar voice neared her.

"Lucy," said DC David Evans in his soft Welsh accent. "Did you want me? Phil Henderson said you had a few questions. Lucy Spires asked him to go through details of the previous day, from the time they picked him up in the afternoon, up until they left him this morning. She knew DC

David Evans was a stickler for detail. He went through his notes. He started detailing from his note pad.

"My shift started at five forty-five pm, I met the day shift team, who watched his activities from when he started work around ten am. We met at Three Wood motorway services, Northbound carriageway at five pm. The target Lorry was parked at the far end of the lorry park area. There were no other vehicles parked nearby. We parked our unmarked police car at an excellent vantage point to observe the target lorry." He went on, now with an audience of the rest of the team listening in, in case they picked up anything missed.

He continued, "I was joined by DC Vicki Wallace to give me back up support. A little after five-fifteen pm, we observed our target leaving the lorry, walking to a busy service area, buying a meal, eating it; then he bought a bottle of still water, slowly drinking the water as he walked back to the lorry. Not to alert him he was under surveillance, we waited until nightfall. We discreetly took turns to look around his lorry. There were sounds of either music or a television in the lorry cab. We couldn't see in as it was too high and he had drawn the cab curtains for his privacy." The room was now in total silence. DC David Evans looked around, the familiar faces hanging on his words. "The lorry never budged. At six minutes past one, our target walked across to the now quiet services. We saw him walking across, and myself and Vicki Wallace got into the area first. He went straight to the retail shop and asked the attendant for a shower key.

"From there he went to the 'Male' toilets, walked into a cubicle, locked it, but I heard him have a pee! The whole toilet block was empty. He didn't need to go in there. He didn't see me as I was around a corner from him, but I clearly heard him. A few minutes later, he had a shower for fifteen minutes, and came out wearing a different coloured T shirt. He must have changed into fresh clothes after his shower. A couple of things to note. He asked the shop attendant for the time and yet he was wearing a watch on his left wrist. It confused me, also I would have thought he would need a drink as he bought his last one around six pm, however he purchased nothing when he went for his shower. He walked back to his lorry. I'm sure he was whistling while he walked. We couldn't get too close as he may have seen me and DC Wallace. At six am, his lorry started up and a minute or so later, he went on his way to start deliveries." He paused after that. Lucy Spires thought the team were about to applaud him on his detailed account of his observations.

Lucy Spires considered his words for a minute. "Dave," she said, "why on earth would you ask what time it was when you already wore a watch?"

He came straight back with, "Well Ma'am, sorry I mean Lucy, I thought that strange, but then thought his watch battery had gone, or he'd damaged his watch and it was broken, or had fallen asleep, woke up and felt he needed a wash. It seemed an odd time to have a shower, at one am." Lucy Spires again collected her thoughts.

"I agree, a shower at that time of night is hard to explain, but my biggest query is why he just didn't urinate in the stand-up male urinals. Why did he feel the need to use a locked toilet cubicle?" The noise in the room began to rise as everyone returned to what they were doing before DC David Evans came in. Lucy Spires felt she was missing something. What, she just couldn't put her finger on it.

A few minutes later, Detective Chief Inspector Toby Butler came into the busy room. He stood near his office door.

"Everyone," he said in a loud voice, again. "Everyone. We have a name for our victim of this morning's unlawful killing" He lifted up a piece of paper nearer his nose. "Miss Gillian Hepple, twenty-nine years old. No previous, but on a drug rehabilitation programme, a regular class one drug user. Her next of kin, her brother Stephen Hepple, informed us she lost an aunty who brought her up as her parents split up when she was seven. Both parents didn't want her, so her aunt took her and her brother in. Reported her missing at eight am this morning. Positive ID at one-thirty this afternoon. Her life was taken between midnight and one am, in the same way as the other victims, strangled while on her knees. Again, the home office pathologist feels the position she was in means, in his opinion, that she was performing oral sex. There was evidence of intercourse. Semen samples were sent off to the lab for possible identification and a high level of drugs were in her system. Any questions, my door is open." With that he turned around. Lucy Spires heard the door swish open and its occupant heave a loud sigh as he slumped into his chair.

"Emma," said Lucy Spires, "Where are you?"

With that DC Emma Harper was at her side. She put her hand on her arm. "I have to see Butler now!" she said as she stood up. DC Emma Harper guided Lucy Spires to the entrance of his office door.

"Sir, do you have a minute?" asked DC Emma Harper. He gestured for the two to enter. Lucy Spires stood in front of his desk.

"Toby, too many questions, no answers, but hear me out. Last night, why did our suspect target park so far away from the entrance to the motorway services. It was a cool night and he could have parked twenty yards away. Instead he must have been around four hundred yards, if our two detectives could see him get out of his lorry, go towards the shop, leave their car and still get inside before him. Why park there when the lorry park was sparsely busy? Point two, why use a cubicle? Unless he was hiding something. Point three, why a shower at the early hours of the morning. You would have a shower when you've been asleep to freshen you up. Point four, why ask a shop assistant for the time when a clock is clearly visible on a wall in front of you and you are wearing a bloody watch. Unless you want the assistant to remember you and the time you were there. Point five, why whistle while you walk back to a lorry? Unless you are in a very good mood. I wouldn't be in a happy place if I had just had a hot shower and had a long walk in cold air to sleep in a lorry. Point six, poor Gillian Hepple lost her life less than eight miles from the motorway service station! I'm sorry Toby, but this is our man. The lorry is the key!"

As she said that, she realised tears were rolling down her face. Toby stood up. He passed Lucy Spires a paper tissue from a box at the side of his desk. Lucy Spires remained in her pose, standing in front of the desk.

"Lucy," said the man opposite. "That is an argument I have nothing to come back with. Emma, get Phil Henderson and take yourselves to the 'Shopwell Tyres/ depot and have a closer look at both our suspect and the lorry he cares enough to take home and bloody polish. I'll let our Chief Constable know our new line of enquiry." With that, he sat down and picked up his desk phone. He looked up. "Ladies, what are you waiting for? Please close the door when you leave!"

Lucy Spires' heart was pounding in her chest. DC Emma Harper guided Lucy Spires towards DC Phil Henderson. Lucy Spires quickly went through the details she had told Detective Chief Inspector Butler. He sprang to his feet, ready for action. Lucy Spires lifted a hand and spoke. "Can we take a marked police car? If our man is there, I want him to know who we are. I want him to feel uncomfortable from the second we arrive!"

DC Phil Henderson made a quick call to the police garage. He had always liked driving marked police vehicles as every driver adhered to every letter of the highway code when they were around.

Chapter 10

The two detectives and Lucy Spires drove to the 'Shopwell Tyre' depot. On the way through traffic, Chief Constable James Ingram rang DC Emma Harper to tell her he had sent further police officers to support in case needed. He had spoken to his new 'friend', the managing director of 'Shopwell Tyres'. He would give them as much help as possible. The drivers were returning following delivering stock to their customers. Lucy Spires asked DC Phil Henderson to park the police car in full vision of the employees of the tyre company. Before they got out of their police car, Lucy Spires asked to go straight to the target vehicle. Identify their target suspect Richard Edward Garner, keep watching him, and she said he must be kept away from the vehicle. She also asked DC Phil Henderson to keep the owners away from the parked lorries and keep them busy and away from any interfering. He agreed to do this as he trusted Lucy Spires' judgement completely, although what he was going to say he didn't know.

Phil Henderson led them into the workshop where there were four lorries parked, all reversed into the building. The lorry at the end of the row was the suspect one. He double checked the registration number with police headquarters. They confirmed it was indeed the target vehicle. Phil Henderson went through a glass door with a sign above it saying 'Office – Private'. He had his identification card in his hand. Lucy Spires and DC Emma Harper waited near the lorries. DC Emma Harper looked around. She could see a half dozen faces looking through a window from a room to the left of the office where DC Phil Henderson was talking to a man in a smart suit and a younger man, also smartly dressed. She took them to be the managing director and his son. The six faces peering through the glass looked like they were indeed drivers and warehouse staff. Three had mugs in their hands, and one had a newspaper. The other two looked as though they were using mobile phones. Phil Henderson came out of the office, putting his ID wallet in his jacket pocket as he walked toward them.

"The MD and his son are only too pleased to help us with our enquiries. There is still a vehicle due back anytime, but it's a pickup truck, used for very local jobs. We have free reign to look at all the vehicles. Our Chief Constable wants his help in eliminating them from our ongoing investigations."

With that, DC Emma Harper led them both to the back of the lorries. The end vehicle was the one of most interest. The lorries had hydraulic tail lifts, all on the floor, presumably ready to be loaded for the following day. Lucy Spires and DC Emma Harper stepped onto the tail lift of the end lorry.

"Going up?" asked Phil Henderson as the tail lift jerked into life and the two girls were lifted around four feet from the ground. Lucy Spires held onto the side as they rose up. She felt a little queasy. When the lift had stopped, Lucy Spires walked into the empty space. The smell of rubber from the tyres was all around. She walked slowly further into the lorry. She turned to face her friend.

"Emma, please tell me what the staff in the room next to the office are doing?" she said.

DC Emma Harper spun slowly around. She glanced then turned back facing Lucy Spires. "Ok, two are playing on mobile phones, one is reading a newspaper, the other three are not looking toward us, having a hot coffee by the look of them. Why do you ask?"

Lucy Spires then walked towards the front of the empty lorry. She stopped when she felt a wooden wall in front. The smell of rubber was stronger here. She thought the warm sunshine would have made the rubber tyres warm up, hence the smell. But there was something else, something she couldn't quite explain that was wrong. She felt her way back toward the rear door. She counted her steps. Twelve in total. When she reached the back of the lorry, she heard Phil Henderson talking to the two gentlemen from the office about tyres for his daughter's car and moaning how he would end up paying for them. Lucy Spires felt her way toward DC Emma Harper, who took hold of Lucy Spires' arm as she was near the edge. Lucy Spires moved her head nearer to DC Emma Harpers.

She whispered, "Emma, please look over my shoulder and tell me if any of the six have changed or moved."

Again, DC Emma Harper looked through the dusty glass, over the shoulder of Lucy Spires. She took a breath and said, "The one reading the paper hasn't moved. Two are washing up cups, one is talking to a colleague while still looking at his phone, and the other is still on his phone."

Lucy Spires asked her friend to pretend to make a phone call while watching the men at the same time. DC Emma Harper did as she was told. She discreetly pretended to be talking on her mobile while watching the men. Lucy Spires again walked towards the front of the lorry. The rubber smell was stronger the further she went, but there was something else, something wrong. She couldn't work it out. She again paced to the rear of the lorry. DC Emma Harper unprompted turned towards her friend.

"Lucy, the newspaper reader hasn't blinked, hasn't turned a page and is staring at your every movement. The other five are going about their business in a completely normal way. I think one of them, washing up their mugs has broken one, the others are laughing and joking. Our newspaper reader has not moved a muscle." Her voice was trembling as she finished her sentence.

Lucy Spires felt for her friends' arm and squeezed gently. "Time to go down now," said Lucy Spires.

DC Emma Harper pressed a button with a downward arrow on it. The tail lift stuttered for a second then with a bump, the tail lift was on the floor. Lucy Spires still held her arm.

She said softly, "Is newspaper reader on his feet?"

"No, he hasn't moved. He is staring at us," came the reply.

Lucy Spires felt the side of the lorry. It felt smoother than the inside roughness of the wood panelling. She asked her friend again to watch the reactions through the window as she paced up and down the outside of the lorry. As she neared the front of the lorry, she had the unnerving feeling something wasn't right. She walked to the end of the lorry, just before the cab part of it and let her hand slide along the side as she counted her steps from front to back. She did this twice to make sure she hadn't miscounted. On the inside, she had taken twelve steps, but on the outside, she had taken almost fourteen. Then she realised the thing that was nagging at the back of her mind. She could smell rubber, obviously from tyres, but there was also the smell of petrol.

Lucy Spires could hear Phil Henderson talking rubbish. He had done a great job, as he was asked. Lucy felt along to the rear of the lorry. She reached out for Emma's arm.

"Emma," said Lucy Spires. "Get our lads in here now. Call for back up as I think newspaper reader may turn violent." With that DC Emma Harper took out of her pocket her police radio and called in the car full of officers into the building.

The two owners stood looking at the swarming officers running into the building. DC Emma Harper took charge,

"Lads, over here please."

Five uniformed officers came and stood before the two women, joined by a smiling Phil Henderson. Lucy Spires told the police officers to keep everyone where they were. She gestured to DC Phil Henderson to come close to her.

"Phil," said Lucy Spires, "I don't think I'm wrong, but if you come with me, you can help to prove me right."

With that she stepped onto the tail lift. DC Phil Henderson held Lucy Spires' left arm as he pressed the button with an arrow pointed upwards. The tail lift shuddered again as it lifted the two detectives and Lucy Spires up four feet. It came to a stop. She walked toward the front of the lorry. Confident steps; she knew how many she could take. As she got to the wooden wall, she stopped.

She took a breath and said, "Phil, Emma, behind this wood you should find a black or dark coloured motor cycle with no lights or registration number on it. Plus, I would guess a pair of new leather gloves and a box or a chart containing trophies, earrings from all the girls this coward has murdered."

The two detectives stood speechless. Phil Henderson looked at the way the wooden wall was held in place. There were butterfly type nuts holding up the wall. He undid the top four, then the middle two and two near the base. He was a tall man. He moved the panel. It dropped a little in height, then fell backwards into the empty storage space. DC Emma Harper moved Lucy Spires further back from the wooden panel DC Phil Henderson was lowering down.

Behind was indeed a medium sized black motor cycle, on a stand held at an angle to keep in place. There was bag with a set of black clothes on top of the seat. A small petrol can to the left-hand side, a pair of gloves, used for gardening or DIY covering his wrists. Above that was a pegboard with small jewels taped to it with a little note with a time and a date. At the side of the motor cycle was a small handmade wooden shelf with a wet shaving set, a razor, shaving gel, a pack of moistened toilet tissues and a large opened pack of condoms.

"Lucy," he said, his voice trembling. "We have the murdering bastard! I'm looking at leather gloves, a black motorbike, a full set of biker's leathers, a board with clear taped earrings and a note of times and place of the murders. How on earth did we do this?" His voice fell away. He turned to see Lucy Spires standing, holding on to the wall. Tears were rolling down her face. He walked over and put his hand on her arm. He started to guide Lucy Spires toward the back of the lorry. She put her hand firmly on his, her heart racing. They walked slowly towards a row of uniformed faces, almost all were smiling.

The other officers had watched the events in the back of the lorry unravel. The atmosphere among them became a noisy one as most realised what had just happened.

From nowhere came the scream of a very angry man who tried to fight his way toward the two females. He was stopped in his tracks by four burly uniformed officers.

He kept shouting profanities, screaming, "The whores deserved to die! Every bitch whore deserves my hands on their necks!"

He was very strong. The two uniformed officers were brushed aside. He was intent on stopping his lorry from any further investigation. A team of six policemen manhandled him to the ground. He was trying to lash out, bite, head-butt and still screamed profanities and threats to kill the two female officers with his bare hands.

He was still screaming as he was bundled, his hands behind his back safely handcuffed and moved towards a waiting police car. DC Emma Harper ran towards him. She stopped the officers putting him into the back seat of the car.

She took a deep breath, looked at Lucy Spires and said, "This is for you Lucy. Richard Edward Garner, I am arresting you on suspicion of murder, murders including Julie Ann Cooper, on fifteenth of March, twenty eighteen. You do not have to say anything, but anything you do say may be used against you in a court of law. Do you understand?" She looked at the leading uniformed officer, nodded and within a second he was pushing his head down gently as he went into the back seat of the car.

DC Emma Harper looked at his face through the passenger door window, he had a look of disgust on his face. His brow had drops of sweat from his exertions. He stared at her and banged his forehead twice against the glass. DC Emma Harper smiled as she could see a red mark above his dark, staring eyes. Blue lights flashing, the police car pulled away with three uniformed policemen squeezed into the car along with the suspect.

Dc Emma Harper walked back to Lucy Spires. She put her arms around her and gave her a hug. She could hear DC Phil Henderson breaking the news to Detective Chief Inspector Toby Butler on his mobile. He barely stopped to take a breath. This was the biggest case he had ever been involved in. DC

Emma Harper held Lucy Spires for a further few seconds. They parted, Lucy Spires still holding her friend's arm. DC Emma Harper looked around for her colleague, DC Phil Henderson, who was walking toward them.

He said, "The whole team have sent their congratulations. DCI Butler is absolutely delighted. I don't think we could make him any happier. He wants our statements on his desk by nine tomorrow morning. Chief Constable Ingram has personally sent his thanks. We have all made a difference and brought something to solving this case."

After all the mayhem, more officers arrived. She could hear various voices as the officers were taking statements from the employees of 'Shopwell Tyres'. She heard the managing director and his son talking about the suspect they'd just arrested. They were so shocked and trusted this man. She heard them say he was the perfect employee. He was never late, was the last man to leave. His customers thought he was a genuine friend to most of them. He'd even told the managing director he was to join a choir at his local church to help a few elderly neighbours out and take them along with him. He even took his lorry home some weekends to clean and polish it on his own time as he wanted to represent the company in such a good way.

DC Emma Harper took hold of her arm. "Chief Constable Ingram wants to speak to you. He's got the press on his back and he's preparing a statement," she said, putting her mobile in her hand.

"Ex Detective Chief Inspector Lucy Spires!" he said slowly. "What can I say. How the hell did you fathom this out? The whole police headquarters is talking about you. What gave you your breakthrough?"

Lucy Spires brushed the wetness from her face and took a deep breath. "Well," she began. "I knew it must be our man. I don't do coincidences. There were too many things that led to him. Being unable to see and being distracted, I went over the pieces again and again. I came to the conclusion the lorry was the key. A vehicle can't be in two places at the same time. But if you are clever, the driver can. I went through all the statements. There were snippets of information. The motorcycle, seen a few times, he free-wheeled quietly. Why? The way he killed these women. The trophies he took from them, they couldn't be larger ones for storage. The dates of the offences were too close not to be important with the CCTV sightings. Then, when I got onto the target vehicle, I could smell petrol. My father had a moped when I was growing up. The smell of two stroke petrol filled our garage constantly, so I knew it had to be a petrol driven motorcycle. I counted my steps inside the lorry, then counted them from the outside. There had to be a false wall, with what was hidden behind I wasn't quite sure what we would find. Then I realised exactly where he parked his lorry in the motorway services was a key piece of evidence. He parked the lorry there to use the motorway service station service road. This is the road used for deliveries for the shop, restaurants and emergency vehicles. They are never used at night, no CCTV needed and links to all routes. Our man would open the panel in his lorry, take out his motorcycle, free-wheel out of earshot, go to the woman, do what he did and return the same way.

"There was no DNA to pick up as he shaved all his hair off and always used a condom. I realised this when I heard his work nickname of 'Hairless Reg'. I just put these pieces of the jigsaw together. They fitted and that is why I knew it could only be this man. Sir, you have no idea how good this feels!" With that, she took the phone from the side of her head, passed it to DC Emma Harper, who terminated the call.

Lucy Spires had never felt so tired. She turned to her friend. "Emma, will you take me home? I'm shattered. But will you please go via chicken in a bucket! I'm absolutely famished!"

DC Emma Harper laughed out loud. The butterflies racing around her body were starting to settle down. Taking a good friend to share a large amount of fried chicken would be a pleasure. The circus of the police team was left behind as they drove away. Forensics were busy taking photographs of every inch of the lorry. Both didn't speak as until they reached the home of Lucy Spires. They went in and went through the whole case.

This was the first major case DC Emma Harper had been a major part of. She hoped it would not be her last. She had planned a long and progressive career. She also wanted a family. She came from a large family: a sister and two brothers. Her father worked as a hospital porter and her mother as a library assistant. Both were surprised at her career choice, but she really enjoyed the police force. Every day is different, with fresh challenges and working with a fantastic number of people she thought.

Lucy Spires later said goodbye to her friend. She was to pick her up at eight o'clock the following morning to complete her statement. She wondered if this was to be her final contribution, her final case. She knew she would see Chief Constable James Ingram in less than twelve hours. She wondered if he would ask for her help again, or would she live in her total darkness alone. There was one final case she would like to close, that of Farooq El Haj. He was the person who caused her blindness. As she was still alive, she was the loose end he should have cleared up. She knew this man, knew how evil he was, and knew how much suffering he brought, bringing in his cache of drugs, bringing in people illegally. She had time to plan how to bring this man to justice. She knew his secrets and she had a person on the inside. The only thing she didn't know were the names of the members of all the agencies Farooq El Haj had on his payroll. She knew he kept a book and inside were all the names, contact details, payments made, the reasons they had no choice, but to join his organisation, which meant reasons they would never leave. The file on him was in Lucy Spires' head. She would never read it again, but the knowledge she had would put this man in jail for a very long time.